"I give up

Gwyn gestured in frustration. "You're eating *banana pudding* for breakfast?"

"It's got eggs," Neal protested. "Why do I feel as though I'm talking to my mother?"

She folded her arms. "Number one: because you're talking to someone who cares. And number two: do *I* look like your mother?"

There was a moment of silence, a moment charged with a growing awareness of each other.

"*I* know what's best for me." Neal gestured to his heart.

"Okay, Mr. Sweet-slob, go for it! But when you develop some awful disease, don't forget that someone warned you, once upon a time!" She wheeled around. When she felt his hand on her arm, she stopped.

"Gwyn, hold it. You're absolutely right." He grinned, his old keep-out facade unconsciously slipping. "I'm up Harmony Creek without a paddle. Rescue me...."

And with those words, his hand moved from her arm to draw her into a tight embrace.

Mary Tate Engels was inspired to include the "bridge to nowhere" theme in *The Right Time* after a similar debate occurred near her home in Tucson. When it was proposed that a bridge be built spanning the Santa Cruz River, joining a small retirement community to an expanse of ranch land, many citizens were opposed. Mary decided to revise the situation somewhat for the residents of fictitious Harmony Creek.

She also did a lot of research on time management before creating her heroine. As a result, she says she's organized herself now—"sort of." This is Mary's third Temptation.

Books by Mary Tate Engels

HARLEQUIN TEMPTATION
215—SPEAK TO THE WIND

Writing as Corey Keaton

194—THE NESTING INSTINCT

The Right Time
MARY TATE ENGELS

Harlequin Books

TORONTO • NEW YORK • LONDON
AMSTERDAM • PARIS • SYDNEY • HAMBURG
STOCKHOLM • ATHENS • TOKYO • MILAN

In loving memory of Daddy
...the original Tate,
who knew more about the
Tennessee mountains than
anyone

And special thanks to Toni S.,
who helped me prioritize and organize
for this book

FORTY YEARS OF
Romance

Published March 1989

ISBN 0-373-25343-5

1

HOW COULD HE DO THIS to her? Why *her*? Why now? The chief reason he'd given was "good for your career." But she wasn't convinced.

Gwyn checked her watch. She had just enough time to finish her shopping and pick up her dry cleaning before the meeting Ed had called for one o'clock to make the announcement. He would give details then. But she dreaded it. She didn't really want to know more.

Gwyn Frederick, time management and efficiency expert, pushed through the noon crowd, intent on keeping her schedule. Thirty-eight minutes later she slid into an empty chair in the back of the room that buzzed with the chatter of her twenty-odd colleagues at Mark Time Inc.

Travis Montgomery, former boyfriend and now just friend, shifted and looked over his shoulder, giving her a frown that said, *Thought you wouldn't make it in time.*

Gwyn countered with a competent smile as if to say, *Of course I'm on time. It's my specialty.* She pulled a list from her purse and drew a line through four more items. Sighing with the satisfied sense of accomplishment, she reviewed the remainder of the list, mentally estimating when and where she would attend to the rest of it.

Two minutes later, right on time, Ed Buhler, executive director of Mark Time Inc., entered with a fistful of papers and began handing them out before addressing his young professional staff. "Our meetings in Washington during the past few months have resulted in an exciting development, designed to increase productivity. SHARE is a new program of collaboration between the private sector and federal programs. We have agreed to participate in this innovative concept because . . ."

Gwyn glanced at Travis, rolling her dark brown eyes. *SHARE?*

Travis raised his eyebrows a couple of times in a comic gesture. *Another bureaucratic ploy.*

Gwyn glanced down and spotted a run in her new black stockings. Damn! It was the first time she'd worn them. She nervously fluffed one side of her thick brunette hair, wishing Ed would simply get the announcement over with.

" . . . pleased to announce that Gwyn Frederick has been chosen as the first from our company to participate." Ed smiled at her and paused for the smattering of applause.

Finally. Gwyn acknowledged the response with a tight smile, the run in her hose forgotten. Chosen? She knew why they were applauding—because they weren't "chosen."

Ed continued. "SHARE is an acronym for Special Help Assists and Rewards Everyone. Basically it means that private businesses offer short-term consulting to government organizations struggling and on the verge of collapse. In effect, our goal is to help them run people-oriented companies with a better business sense. The point to this whole program is that we're doing it to help people, not to sustain a failing bureaucracy. I guarantee you that work on this project will be rewarding, although it isn't for glory. It's two weeks doing your SHARE."

Gwyn's mouth dropped open. Two weeks? She'd figured one, max.

Someone posed a question about salaries.

"Don't worry," Ed answered. "We weren't asking for your complete sacrifice, just your expertise. Your salary will continue just as if you were here. Think of it as a business trip. This is a donation of time from the company. Essentially we are donating you. Your only responsibility is to go out there and do your best. It's sort of a business-oriented Peace Corps."

After fielding a few more questions, Ed asked Gwyn to join him in his office, and dismissed the general meeting. Two minutes later she was sitting across the desk from him, disturbed but controlled.

"Why me? When? Where? Why two weeks?"

He leaned forward with a smile on his ruddy face. "It's a great opportunity for you to show your versatility, Gwyn. I have respect for you and your ability. That's why I chose you first." He folded large forearms on his desk.

She purposely slowed her speech. "What did I do to deserve this, Ed?"

"You're good at what you do. I trust you to be a good rep for the company."

Gwyn leaned forward. "Come on, Ed. The real reason."

"Because this one is located in a southern region and you're from the South."

"Attending Vanderbilt University in Nashville for four years doesn't qualify me as a Southerner. That's the extent of my experience in the South."

"That's good enough for me. It's more than anyone else around here."

She took a deep breath. Obviously there was no way out of this. "So what's the job?"

"Simple. You could do it with your eyes shut. Organize a little rural health clinic in eastern Tennessee." He started shoving papers around on his desk, searching for something. "I have more info here somewhere."

"It's Appalachia, isn't it?"

"Just on the fringes. Just barely." Ed stopped and looked at her. "Well, you didn't expect to reorganize the National Health System, did you?"

She twisted her purse strap. "When?"

"Soon. You'll leave in a week."

"A week?" She felt herself becoming increasingly agitated. "That'll be December! It's a busy time for me."

"I know. It's busy for everyone, Gwyn. But we needed to schedule something with this program before the end of the year. Anyway, you're so organized you won't have any trouble." He continued pawing through the mess on his desk. "You'll be back in plenty of time for Christmas."

"But there's shopping and a million—"

"You have a week to do it before you go. Heck, they say the best shopping day is the day after Thanksgiving. Do it all then."

"And the most crowded."

"Aha! Here it is!" With a satisfied smile he pulled out a manila envelope and handed it to her. "I knew it was here somewhere. Now listen, Gwyn. I realize you have doubts about this. But trust me. I'm doing you a favor. This is a cinch job, a choice assignment. You'll do it easily, come back and file a report with the board. It'll look good on your record."

Don't do me any more favors, she thought miserably. "And it's a good tax deduction for the company."

"A little tax deductible goodwill never hurt anyone." He shrugged his burly shoulders. "Trust me, kid. I won't steer you wrong."

Gwyn looked down at the packet in her hands. Her peripheral vision caught the glaring run in her dark stocking. Some things couldn't be helped or altered, like the rip in her hose and this assignment. "Well, what's two weeks? It'll probably go quickly."

"That's the spirit. Your itinerary is in the envelope. Flight's already scheduled. But if the time isn't okay, check with Sandra. She'll fix you up right. I think you fly into Chattanooga, get a bus to someplace like, uh, Ducktown, where someone will meet—"

"A bus?" Gwyn could feel her temperature rising. "*Duck*town? Where the heck—"

"Beats me. There's a map in your packet. It'll explain."

"Ducktown. I don't believe this. How could you do this to me, Ed?" She shook her head. She tried to be a good sport, had always been a company person. But there were times . . .

"Remember the good hardworking people who'll benefit from your work, Gwyn." He winked and stood, extending his hand, signifying an end to their meeting.

She followed suit. "Yeah. Not for glory. I think I'm supposed to say thanks."

"You've got class, Gwyn."

And a run in my new hose, along with a crummy assignment and a million-odd things to do. "You really should straighten up that mess on your desk, Ed. Want me to get you organized?"

"Touch a scrap on this desk and you die."

"Right. You realize it's bad business not to practice what you preach."

"I know where everything is, and I don't need you telling me about my business. Oh, and Gwyn, happy Thanksgiving."

"Sure. You, too."

She left his office clutching her purse and the manila packet. Having accepted the inevitable, the so-called choice assignment, Gwyn wondered if she'd have time to do everything on her list before she left the vibrant Second City for . . . Ducktown.

GWYN AND TRAVIS PUT their heads together over a road map of Tennessee. He circled an area with a red marker. "Here it is, in the middle of nowhere."

"How do you get there?" With her finger Gwyn traced several winding lines representing the road system that seemed to dwindle to nothing.

"You can't get there from anywhere," he joked. "They'll drop you in by helicopter. It's getting out that's the trick. You have to stand on this big flat rock and wave—"

"All right! I can do without your misguided humor."

"Think of it as an adventure, Gwyn."

"Which I want like a hole in the head!" She rolled her eyes. "You know I don't like any more adventure than I get watching *Romancing the Stone*."

"It can't be that bad. Plus Ed's right. It'll look good on your résumé."

"I don't care about my résumé right now. I have to deal with the immediate. Will you help me get everything done before I leave, Travis? Of all weeks . . ." She gestured in the air with an open hand as she paced her cubicle.

Travis leaned against her desk and gave her a sympathetic look. "Sure. I'll be glad to."

"Why now, of all times?" she moaned.

"Murphy's Law."

"I hate it. And I hate people who blame Murphy's Law. Where's my list?" She opened her purse and pulled out her day-planner.

"Let's take it one step at a time," he said calmly. "What is absolutely necessary?"

Gwyn loved Travis's organizational ability. He quickly gained perspective by putting things in order of their priority. She teasingly called him "Mr. Efficient."

She gazed steadily at him. "Travis, it isn't the office work. It's . . . it's personal."

"Oh. Well, you don't have to tell me."

"No, I mean, my problems center around my family."

"Hmm," he said with a mock-serious nod. "We all have those. Problems and families. And problems with families."

"Dammit, Travis, be serious! My time is limited. Next week is Thanksgiving . . ."

"That usually occurs on the last Thursday and Friday in November."

"You don't understand. I have to contribute to the turkey dinner. Everybody in our family brings something so one person doesn't have the full load."

"Sounds reasonable to me."

"Each year our family keeps getting bigger. Somebody either gets married or has another baby." Gwyn gave him a weary look. "I'm supposed to bring pies."

He hooted with laughter. "Ahh, now I understand your problem. You can't make a pie."

She didn't smile. "Not worth a spit. I figure I'll need at least six pies, maybe seven for that crowd." She slumped into her chair and propped her chin on her fist. "I know it's a sacrilege, but I'm seriously considering buying them. I don't have time to experiment with pies, especially now."

"Of course you should buy them," Travis said, deciding quickly. "Your family will understand. After all, you're a working woman. They can't expect you to do everything."

"My mother never bought a pie in her life."

"Why didn't you tell her you couldn't make the pies?" he demanded logically. "Mashed potatoes are so much easier."

"I wasn't there when they decided who'd bring what. And I . . ." Gwyn shrugged.

"Couldn't admit it." He folded his arms and nodded slowly. "Okay, the pies are solved. You'll buy them. In fact, there's a great little bakery around the corner from my apartment. I use it all the time. I'll be glad to pick them up for you."

She smiled, somewhat relieved. "Thanks, Travis."

"Okay, what next?"

Gwyn glanced down her list. "There's all my Christmas shopping and my parents' twenty-ninth wedding anniversary party two days after Thanksgiving."

Travis raised both hands and began to retreat from the room. "Shopping isn't my bag, Gwyn. And your parents' wedding anniversary is definitely too personal for me. You order the pies and I'll pick them up. And I'll do anything around here. But the rest is yours."

"Chicken," she mumbled, not even looking up when he left.

THE NEXT WEEK was a whirlwind. Gwyn couldn't do enough fast enough. She utilized every spare hour, every small chunk of time, every brief moment. By the time she had fulfilled her obligations for Thanksgiving dinner, she went home with a headache and vowed never to eat again. Well, maybe in six months.

Shopping was no better. She and her sister-in-law battled the day-after-Thanksgiving crowds to get the best bargains and ended up arguing at lunch over a matter so trivial that Gwyn had forgotten the details by the time she called Celeste the next day to apologize.

The Frederick family gathering for their parents' anniversary on Sunday was a disaster. Celeste and Bob and their three children arrived late. Gwyn's youngest sister, Angie, and her new husband, Andrew, argued throughout the meal. Finally their mother, who never argued with anyone, asked them to take their problems home and not spoil her anniversary. But it was spoiled, anyway.

By the time Gwyn boarded the plane for her flight south, she was exhausted and, frankly, glad to be leaving. When she arrived in Atlanta, she felt content that she was almost there. Little did she realize that the flight had been the shortest, or least complicated, leg of an arduous journey. There was the commuter flight to Chattanooga, the bus to Cleveland, then two transfers before she stumbled down the bus steps at her destination.

Ducktown. She'd lost track of time and direction and only knew for sure that it was nearly dark and pouring rain; that she was cold, tired, and hungry; and that she wasn't there yet.

Gwyn huddled beneath an overhang on the landing of a long-abandoned railroad station in what she considered must be a ghost town. And waited. All the while she privately cursed everything, from the cold, dreary weather to various opinions of Ed Buhler, to her job at Mark Time Inc., lady luck, and even efficient Travis, who'd had the poor taste to joke about this trip.

Finally, out of the hazy mist, two headlights appeared. Her heart leaped with gratitude, and she almost ran out to meet them. An old man approached her sheltered spot, wearing overalls and a tattered felt hat pulled down over his ears. He looked like someone out of *The Waltons*, circa 1930.

"Howdy," he drawled, touching the soaking-wet brim of his hat. "You the Yankee nurse goin' to Harmony Crick?"

Between them a waterfall drained from the roof and she strained to see and hear him.

"I'm Gwyn Frederick from Mark Time, and yes, I'm going to Harmony Creek Clinic." She had to speak loud over the sound of the rain on the wooden platform. "But I'm not a nurse."

"You from Chicago?"

"Yes."

"I reckon you're the one then. 'Specially since you're the only one here."

"Are you . . ." She lifted a crumpled piece of paper containing names and addresses and scribbled bus routes. "Are you Mr. McPherson?"

"Yep, that's me. Folks call me Jed." He chuckled. "Well, if you're you and I'm me, I guess we'd better hitch 'er up. We've got a ways to go."

"We do? You mean we aren't there yet?" Gwyn imagined the luxury of a warm room, a bowl of hot soup, a steaming shower and a clean bed. Sometimes one settled for simple pleasures. And gladly. "Could you just drop me off at the local hotel? I'll go to the clinic tomorrow."

Jed chuckled again, his voice making a strange, crackly sound. "There's no hotel around here, Missy." He reached for her gray-and-burgundy Gucci bags. They were already blotched by rain and mud. "You'll have to stay at the clinic if you stay anywhere at all."

She wondered why he would think she was a nurse. But she quickly shrugged it off, since this whole day had been tiring and unexpected. Gwyn took a deep breath and dashed after her overall-clad chauffeur, wondering if she'd landed in *Hee Haw* instead of the equally nebulous Ducktown.

"Half the stores are boarded up or closed," Gwyn commented as they chugged through the quiet, dark streets in Jed's ancient pickup. "Aren't there any businesses here?"

"Nothing but a combination hardware and drugstore. The post office is in the general store."

"What happened to the town?"

"Hard times. It used to be a busy place, until the mines closed." Jed turned a corner, and they were immediately out of town. And on the way to Harmony Creek.

Since Jed was a man of few words and Gwyn was too tired to think of any scintillating conversation, they lapsed into silence. Gwyn settled back for the trip. But there was no relaxing for her. They bounced for twenty minutes over one of the roughest paved roads Gwyn had ever traversed.

Finally they turned into a bumpy driveway, and the headlights illuminated a large, rambling building and the Harmony Creek Clinic sign. Gwyn had never been so glad to see a place in her life. Immediately the front door swung open, and in the warm yellow glow from inside the room the tall, lean figure of a man was outlined. She could see a fireplace flickering a welcome. Without hesitation she rushed from the damp truck, through the cold rain and into the inviting haven.

She acknowledged a hurried introduction with the occupant, Dr. Neal Perry, bid Jed a brief thank-you and stood shivering before the fire while the doctor shook Jed's hand and walked out on the porch to wave goodbye. When the man returned and closed the door, Gwyn looked closely at him for the first time. And she realized what a fool thing she had done by coming here. They were in the middle of nowhere and apparently alone.

Dr. Perry was devastatingly dark and handsome beneath a full beard and mustache. About six-one and lanky, he wore tight jeans, a pullover with a blue-and-white Nordic design and thermal socks with no shoes. His eyes, sharply contrasting with his sable hair, were strikingly blue, almost matching the cobalt in his sweater.

He stuffed his hands in his pockets and gave her a relieved smile. "Boy, am I glad to see you."

"This place looks like heaven," she responded in a soft, weary voice.

"How was your trip?"

"Long."

"I can imagine." Seeing her up close, quivering as she stood in front of the fireplace, Neal experienced a rush of honest-to-gosh appreciation for the woman. She was attractive, undoubtedly younger than his thirty-one years, with a vulnerability in her chocolate-brown eyes. Her ecru skin had a luminous, healthy glow. Thick brunette hair, stylishly curly and tousled, gleamed in the firelight like rich mahogany. She was slender and of medium height. Her navy pin-striped suit was wrinkled at the hip line, and her matching pumps were speckled with mud.

"Sorry I couldn't pick you up, but I didn't have time. That's why I sent Jed after you."

She gazed around. "You're quite isolated here, Dr. Perry."

"We're also very informal. Please call me Neal."

"Okay, Neal. I'm Gwyn."

"I hope you're prepared to work hard, Gwyn. I can't tell you how badly I need a nurse. We have our share of traumas and deliveries, and I've also scheduled inoculations during the next two weeks while you're here to help. We need so much." He sighed and continued, unable to stop the frustrated flow of words. "The supply cabinet is a shambles, and I think we're out of everything. Also, there needs to be some kind of system for reordering. I have absolutely none. It's catch-as-catch-can around here."

Gwyn frowned and shook her head. "Apparently you and Jed are under the same misconception, Neal. I'm not a nurse. But I can leave you organized, with several helpful systems in place. I guarantee I'll have your office running efficiently in no—"

"Whoa. Just a minute. What do you mean, you aren't a nurse? That's what I requested." The gratitude and smile were suddenly gone from his face.

"I'm in time management."

Neal's ears rang as a flush of anger raced through him. "In what?"

Gwyn took a shaky breath. She didn't like the tone of his voice, or the startled expression on his face. "I work for Mark Time Inc., a company that specializes in improving time efficiency. My area is time as it relates to motion, that is, necessary movement around an office required to get the jobs done. I'm usually assigned the smaller offices, like yours."

"Mine's real small. My nurse quit six months ago, one day after I arrived. I didn't even know where the sterilizer was. And I stay so busy I don't have time to arrange anything." He hooked his thumbs in the belt loops of his jeans. "I expected someone in the health field."

Gwyn noticed the size of his hands and that he wore no wedding ring. "Sorry I can't fill those shoes."

"Mm-hmm." He ran his hand around the back of his neck and turned away with a heavy sigh. "Damned bureaucratic screwup. I can't for the life of me understand their logic. I need medical assistance, and they send me an office clerk."

"Excuse me, Doctor, but I'm not a clerk." Gwyn stopped abruptly as her predicament became agonizingly clear. Her throat constricted, and tears stung her weary eyes. She'd spent a grueling week getting ready for this assignment, traveled seemingly forever to reach this remote spot, was cold, hungry, tired, and now found herself unwanted. Suddenly she felt the urge to throw something. At the good doctor! Or cry. She forced aside both notions and evaluated the situation. He didn't need her; he needed a nurse. If she'd only known, she could have saved him a bunch of trouble and herself the lost time.

Oh, dear, surely she wasn't going to cry!

"H-how did this happen?" Gwyn managed to sound calm and professional. There must be something they could do about the problem. *Remain rational*, Ed always instructed. *The solutions are there. Your job is to find them.* "If you requested medical help, why would they send someone with my skills?"

"I'm asking myself the same question. Typical government snafu. You ask for one thing, and they send what they want you to have."

"You must have requested—"

"I didn't!"

Gwyn folded her arms and felt her professional facade slipping. "You aren't the only one frustrated tonight, Doctor. At least you didn't leave your family and friends at the busiest time of year for some yahoo hollow in the Smoky Mountains. You haven't traveled for ten miserable hours through a cold, driving rain over some of the worst roads imaginable to get to the most remote place you've ever seen, only to find that you aren't the right one and, furthermore, not even wanted. And all I have to look forward to is retracing that same miserable journey tomorrow."

His blue eyes flashed in response to her emotional tirade. "Do you think this is my hometown? I'm here alone. And no, I haven't traveled today. I've only been up since dawn to deliver a baby who decided not to come until noon, when I had ten patients in the waiting room, a kid with a broken arm and an eighty-five-year-old asthmatic with bronchitis who needed to be hospitalized. While I ran—quite literally—from one to the other, I kept thinking how nice it would be tomorrow when I had help."

"And it isn't going to be nice at all, right? If this is a contest to determine whose troubles are greater, I suppose you'd win, Doctor. I certainly can't top babies and the elderly sick." She turned her back on him and held her hands before the fire. "All I know is that I'm tired and hungry." Gwyn realized she sounded petulant, but she didn't care. Frustration and misery dominated her at the present.

He was quiet for a few moments. "Excuse me. I forgot my Southern manners. Jed's wife, Mae, sent over some food for our honored guest. I guess you're it." He moved across the room.

"I'm starved," she admitted with a little sigh.

Neal banged a few pans around. "Someone gave me a quart of apple cider. Do you like it warm?"

"Anything sounds good right now."

An uneasy silence fell between them. Gwyn inspected the large space that served as both kitchen and living room. Two plump chairs and a sofa framed the fireplace, creating a homey atmosphere. The furniture was hand-me-down quality, bits and pieces accumulated rather than chosen to match.

Each wall contained at least one door, indicating this was a central room. The kitchen had an old refrigerator and stove, a large folding table, a sink and a metal cupboard.

The doctor brought two steaming cups of cider and extended one of them toward her. "Sorry. I didn't mean to blast you. I realize it's not your fault. I'm taking my frustrations out on the wrong person. Truce?"

Gwyn looked up into his intense blue eyes and saw a glimmer of sincerity. She nodded and took the cup. "Of course. I'm not usually this way, either. My reaction to all this hasn't been the best. Truce." She sipped the spicy drink. "Thanks. This is great."

He sat in one of the stuffed chairs and gestured for her to take the other one. "The stew and corn bread will be warm in a few minutes."

"Corn bread?" Gwyn lowered herself to the chair opposite him. "I haven't had corn bread in ages. Not since my little grandmother..." She halted. Now was not the time for reminiscence.

His gaze turned soft. So did his voice. "Go on. You had a Southern grandmother?"

Gwyn nodded and a little smile played at the corners of her mouth. "She was short, probably under five feet, and we called her our 'little grandmother.' She was a darling lady from Nashville and influenced my decision to attend Vandy."

"You went to Vanderbilt?"

"In fact, crazy as it sounds, that's why I was chosen for this job. My boss figured that four years in the South was better than nothing. And nobody else in our department had that kind of legacy. I guess he thought it would matter."

"Sound criteria," Neal muttered sarcastically, and shook his head. "I ask for a nurse, not caring if she's from Alaska or Hawaii. Or even if she's a he. They look for someone who's been south of the Mason-Dixon line."

Suddenly, in her exhausted state, the whole thing seemed funny, and Gwyn started laughing. "It's ridiculous. I can't believe I'm here, can't believe places like this exist in this country, can't believe you're for real. I keep thinking I'm going to wake up any minute from this nightmare."

He grinned at her assessment. "Someday I'm sure we'll both chuckle about this mix-up. But I'm afraid it's no dream. Harmony Creek is about as real as it gets. At least, for these parts." He lifted his head sharply and sniffed. "Ahh, the stew's ready."

They ate in silence, both cupping warm bowls of savory stew as they sat opposite each other before the fire. Gwyn could feel herself unwinding, beginning to relax. The food helped, and so did Neal's apology. She noticed the extreme quiet. No sounds but the crackling fire. And it was nice. But she was very tired, and when they finished eating, Neal showed her the room she'd have for the night.

Gwyn stood in the doorway. "It looks like a hospital room."

"You're quick," he said, depositing her blotched-and-wet Gucci bags near the door. "This is for patients who are too ill to travel back home or who need close medical supervision for a few days."

Gwyn walked over to the twin bed. It was the most decorative item in the room, with a country patchwork quilt and hand-embroidered pillow sham.

"Some of my patients fixed this room up. They supplied most of my household goods, in case you hadn't guessed."

"I can tell they're grateful to have a physician way out here."

He shrugged modestly. "I suppose."

"And they were looking forward to a nurse, I'll bet."

"Undoubtedly." He motioned to another door. "Bathroom's in there. Old facilities, but we do have hot running water and flush toilets. And clean towels. Do you need anything?"

She sat on the edge of the bed and rubbed one arm to chase the chill.

"Oh, almost forgot. I have an electric heater for you." He returned in a few minutes and plugged in the small unit. "There. How's that? It has a thermostat on the side."

"Much better. Thanks."

"Anything else?"

"Oh, no . . ." She stood with a small gasp. She'd forgotten, in all this time, to call Travis. He would be waiting to hear from her. "Do you have a phone? I'd like to call home."

"Sorry, but it's been out of order all day. Always is when it rains a lot. Connections are poor. Will your family worry if you don't phone until tomorrow?"

"No. It's okay." She looked at him earnestly. "Neal, I'm sorry things turned out this way. I'll straighten everything out tomorrow."

He nodded and his lips formed a tight smile. "You don't have to apologize, Gwyn. It isn't your fault. Get some rest now. G'night." He turned to leave.

"Uh, Neal?"

He stopped at the door.

"Do you mind if I ask you . . ." She hesitated. "Why in the world are you practicing medicine in such a remote outpost?"

He grinned. "I like it. Nobody bothers me out here."

"Nobody?" She shook her head, perplexed. "Only when they send an organizer from Chicago?"

"Almost nobody," he amended, laughing as he walked away.

The little heater did its job, and so did a hot bath in the deep, old-fashioned tub. Afterward Gwyn felt much better and crawled, relaxed and warm, between the crisp, clean sheets. Her thoughts drifted to the attractive but enigmatic Dr. Neal Perry, keeper of the Smoky Mountain outpost.

What was he doing here? He'd indicated he had no family in Harmony Creek. Or maybe he meant he worked alone.

Although he'd become sharp and abrupt when he discovered she wasn't the right person, he'd shown an ability to be understanding and apologetic.

Beneath his dark hair and beard was a handsome man with beautiful, sensitive eyes the color of the deepest part of the ocean. Intense and almost mysterious. His lean physique was broad shouldered and trim waisted, the kind of body that would be the envy of every paunchy man at the health club back in Chicago—and the idol of every woman. Including her. Oh, no! she objected mentally. She was here to do a job, not to get involved with a client.

FOR THE FIRST TIME since she was a teenager, Gwyn slept until nearly noon the next day. Leaping out of bed, she donned her robe and flew down the hall to the central room. The place smelled like a bakery, due to the numerous cakes and pies lining the long table, apparently gifts from the doctor's admirers. His *many* admirers.

Sipping leftover coffee, Gwyn walked around the room. Noises from beyond a side door indicated it led to Neal's office and clinic. He must be working. She groaned to herself. Well, of course he was. It was midday. It occurred to her that this was the first time she'd been so unproductive in ages. Wasting time, like sleeping in, was not her pattern.

She peered out the window and noted with satisfaction that the rain had stopped. Maybe the phone was working now, so that she could make her necessary phone calls and start her journey home. She dreaded the thought.

Abruptly and in a hurry, Neal entered the room from the side door, dressed in jeans and a plaid flannel shirt with the sleeves rolled halfway up his arms. He grabbed a Coke from the refrigerator before noticing her by the window. "Hi. Sleep okay?"

"Obviously. Why didn't you wake me? I never sleep so late."

"You didn't leave wake-up instructions. Anyway, I figured you needed the rest." He smiled at her, thinking how sexy she looked in her robe, with her hair rumpled and her eyes still sleepy.

"But I've probably lost this whole day because it's so late."

He cut himself a generous slice of cake and started to eat it standing up. "Don't you think you deserve a lost day?"

"I have obligations. I can't afford the time."

"Hmm, have some of Mabel Fry's cake. Fresh coconut and real butter. It's great. And those cinnamon rolls are to die for."

"Cholesterol and sugar for breakfast? How awful."

"It's lunch. You're not one of those health food nuts, are you?" He followed each bite of cake with a swallow of Coke.

"Well, I am calorie conscious." She took a few steps toward him. "Could I use the phone now?"

"Sure. It's working today." Neal finished the cake and dusted his hands over the sink.

He reached inside the door to his office and pulled the phone, which had a long extension cord, into the living room. Then he cut another piece of cake and pretended not to listen as she pleaded and argued with someone named Ed. Eventually she dropped the receiver onto its cradle. She stared out the window for a minute.

"Anything wrong?"

She sighed and looked back at Neal, gesturing weakly at the phone. "My boss. He checked your request form. It lists a nurse first, office help second. They didn't have medical staff available for this program, so they sent office help. He says the company made a commitment that must be upheld by me unless I'm ill. That's a laugh, because you'd probably make me well. Bottom line is that I have to stay two weeks."

"That settles that, I guess." Neal placed the empty Coke bottle under the sink, feeling a sudden elation he couldn't explain. She wasn't the one he needed or wanted, yet he was glad she was here. "I have to get back to work."

"What . . . what am I supposed to do?"

He shrugged. "Anything you want. You can have a two-week vacation for all I care."

Gwyn stared at the door after he'd disappeared through it. Vacation? Here? She refilled her coffee cup and cut herself a hunk of the fresh coconut cake, standing by the window as she ate.

She watched Neal's patients come and go in the muddy parking lot out front. Maybe she could help him by organizing the office. Although medicine wasn't her field, she could learn how to order supplies. She could certainly initiate a few systems to speed the traffic flow and relieve him of mundane or repetitive tasks. That was her expertise.

A young woman with a little child clinging to her skirt helped an old man down the steps in front of the clinic. What the doctor really needed, Gwyn observed, was a nurse. What the *people* really needed was a nurse. How would one go about finding a nurse for such a remote clinic?

She glared at the silent phone with its extension cord that stretched to either the doctor's office or his living quarters. She'd left a message for Travis to call her. Last night she'd wanted desperately to talk to a friend. Ten minutes ago she'd felt obligated to leave him a message. She *should* want to discuss her new job assignment with her co-worker. But she didn't. Strangely she wished he wouldn't bother returning her call.

She finished her cake and coffee and dashed back to the bleak hospital room to get dressed. Gwyn Frederick had things to do today, and she was wasting time.

2

FORTY-FIVE MINUTES LATER Gwyn entered the doctor's office dressed professionally in a suit of pale gray with hose to match and a bluish-gray silk blouse accented with a burgundy paisley scarf. She was ready for work, whatever it was. Or so she thought.

The five patients sitting in the waiting room stared at her, and she became painfully aware of the difference between her appearance and theirs. These were poor people, and they dressed modestly. Which was probably why Neal chose to dress like a lumberjack. He blended with them, while she stood out.

Feeling somewhat uncomfortable, she nodded a mute greeting and assessed the plain room. A cluttered desk near the door and a battered row of metal filing cabinets behind the desk made up the office section. Chairs lined the walls. There were no seating areas with the latest magazines scattered on end tables and pastel prints to soften the decor. Several people stood on the front porch, smoking and chatting. A child whimpered in one of the two examining rooms.

This was not one of Gwyn's usual consulting jobs, and she could see right away that her challenge was great. Taking a deep breath, she considered that even if she only went back with a report of having redecorated the bleak room where sick people waited to see the doctor, she would have accomplished something.

Realistically she also knew that decorating was way down the list of priorities.

When Neal dashed from one of the examining rooms, she grabbed his elbow. "I'd like to talk to you, Doctor."

"Don't have time."

"It won't take long."

He indicated for her to follow him to a tiny room used as a lab and storage area for supplies. "What is it?" He didn't bother looking at her, so she was forced to speak to his broad back.

"I'd like to observe your office routine and procedures."

He glared at her over his shoulder, and she could see the disdain in his expression beneath the beard. "I can't have you slowing me down by getting in my way. These are pretty close quarters here, and I'm really busy."

"I'll stay out of your path. That's how I work."

He sighed and turned back to his business. "You don't have to do this or anything. I won't report you. Go curl up with a book."

"Sorry, I can't abdicate my duty. Anyway, I want to help."

Neal held up a small medicine bottle and filled a syringe. "You mean that your boss ordered you to do something to help 'those po' folks down in Tennessee.' Thanks, but we don't need your kind of help."

"What difference does it make what kind of help you receive? You'll benefit. And so will your patients."

"Are you sure about that?"

"Yes, I am. I'm darned good at what I do, Dr. Perry."

"Then why don't you see if you can organize that front desk? I've got about ten babies to inoculate today, thanks to my having planned on medical help. As if I needed it, I've made my job even busier. Do whatever you want to do. Just stay out of my way. Excuse me."

As Neal slid by her, his shoulder brushed hers, giving her a brief encounter with his strength. His clean, herbal scent lingered for a moment, reminding her of deep forests full of pine trees. He was a stubborn man, though, not pliable like a pine. Obstinate and unbending. Like an oak.

In another minute she heard a child crying, and she knew one more baby had been inoculated against disease. The sound jolted her from thoughts of the man to her goal of making the office better for him and his patients before she left. He'd challenged her to organize his front desk, so that's what she'd do first.

Gwyn started with the scattered files. She could see Neal's handsome face as he dashed from room to room, patient to patient. Those mysterious deep blue eyes of his stood out against the backdrop of his sable hair and beard.

She began to appreciate the doctor as a man pushed to his limits. His was hard work requiring skill, knowledge and a never-ending amount of patience. Her opinion of him rose and somehow made her mundane task of organizing his files more tolerable. She placated herself with the thought that this was a job needing to be done. Anyway, from the corner desk she could study his routines and record her observations.

During the course of the afternoon Gwyn accepted two more cakes, a pie and a deep-dish cobbler for the doctor. Whether the sugary gifts were payment on overdue bills or simply gratitude, Gwyn figured there had to be a better way. She began to work on methods to alter the system and mentioned her suggestions to patients whenever the opportunity arose.

She took incoming calls, made a couple of appointments and relayed messages to the doctor by attaching notes to the next patient's file. Therefore she could communicate with him without interrupting his work flow.

In a brief lull between patients Neal stopped beside the desk. "I've got to hand it to you, Gwyn. You're very efficient."

"It's what I get paid for." She fanned the blank pages of an appointment book with her thumb. "Found it in the bottom drawer. Completely unused. So I made a few appointments for you."

"Why bother?"

"It's called efficiency, Doctor."

"My patients know my system. They sign a book when they enter. I take them on a first come, first served basis around here. And it works."

"If we requested that they make appointments for routine visits, it could speed the process and there wouldn't be all this wasted time waiting to see the doctor. And you would have a more even distribution of patients." She smiled up at him, confident she was already on the path to reorganization.

"But I don't have time to take calls for appointments while I'm seeing patients. I'd rather let them sign in."

"I'll do it for you."

"But you're leaving in two weeks."

"Then we'll have to find someone to take phone calls for you."

"Great. I need a nurse, and you want to hire a receptionist."

"You need them both, Doctor."

"So what else is new?"

"Your records system has broken down. Do you know you have duplicate files here? I've even found some triplicates."

He gave her a mollifying smile and reached inside the top desk drawer. "Here's a list of patients I've seen in the past few weeks with no files. Couldn't find them, although I know they have files somewhere. When I couldn't find the original, I just made another. Didn't have time to hunt."

She took the list. "A computer would solve these problems. You need one desperately."

He placed his palms on the desk and leaned toward her, blue eyes snapping. "I don't think I heard you right. For a minute I thought you said I needed a computer."

"I did." She patted the stack of patient files. "All these could be eliminated, and the information could easily be handled in one machine."

"And who would run the infernal thing?"

"We'll hire someone to run it."

"What other great ideas do you have? Maybe you didn't notice that we're quite isolated. Did you know that some of my patients don't even have phones? And you want to hire someone to run a computer for me? I need a telephone repairman on staff before I need a computer analyst."

Gwyn reached for her pen and began scribbling as he talked. "These are exactly the things I need to know. What are your procedures, your problems, and how can we remedy them?"

He shook his head, a mocking smile of disbelief on his lips. "If you can solve any one of my numerous problems around here, I'll be ecstatic."

"Apparently you don't think I can."

"I do not."

"Well, I'll just have to prove myself, Doctor, because I intend to leave this place better than I found it. That's my job."

He laughed out loud, but there was a cynical tone in his amusement. "I thought the same thing when I first arrived. Then my nurse quit and the sick started coming in faster than I could count, and I settled down to doctoring. Nothing else really matters." He turned away from her as another patient entered the office.

A young mother carried a crying child who seemed to have a head injury. With a few soothing words Neal took the child from the near-frantic mother and went into the first examining room. The mother followed, wringing her hands and sobbing.

Gwyn sympathized with the woman's plight and felt terribly helpless. Neal, however, had been calm and reassuring as he lifted the child in his arms. He was obviously confident in his ability—and just as skeptical of hers.

Since she'd arrived, he'd been generally cranky, cynical and short-tempered. He didn't think she could help any of his situations, didn't even want her help. So why the heck should she bother with this whole mess? Why not curl up with a book as he'd said? Ed would probably never know.

Was it the challenge of the job? Or the challenge of the man? She excused his behavior because she knew him to be frustrated, overworked and probably underpaid. But did that give him the right to behave this way? No, dammit! She gritted her teeth. She'd show him her skills had worth, that her systems had validity.

The phone rang again, and Gwyn began taking a message for the doctor. Another patient, an old man with gnarled hands, entered and signed the registry. His

wrinkled face broke into a toothless grin when he realized he'd be the next patient. "Good timing," she said,
affirming his expectation. "You're next."

"Good luck," the man corrected. "But you know
something? I'd wait to see Doc Perry no matter how
long. This one's the best doctor we've had come down
the pike in a long time."

Gwyn recalled Ed's words when he'd pitched the
program the week before to the room full of well-
dressed yuppies. *This isn't for glory. We're doing it to
help others.* And suddenly her reasons for wanting to
help went beyond her own ego, beyond the man who
served as doctor... to the people.

Her moment of reverie was interrupted by sounds of
the injured child's increased crying accompanied by the
mother's. Due in part to the number of inoculations,
kids had been crying in the clinic all afternoon. Gwyn
had long ago grown weary of the noise. She didn't see
how Neal stood it. He must be exhausted, since he
hadn't stopped even for a coffee break, and the only
food she'd seen him eat were the two hunks of coconut
cake and a Coke. Poor nutrition for such an energetic
job. The doctor probably functioned on a sugar high.

The crying sounded louder as the examining-room
door swung open, and Neal appeared in the doorway.
His face was tense. He looked from Gwyn to the old
man who waited to see him, then back to Gwyn. "I need
some help. Would you—" He motioned for her to come.

"What? Who, me?" Gwyn pointed to herself.

"Yes, please. Hold her for me."

Instinctively Gwyn looked at the old man, then back
to Neal. She shook her head. "But I've had no training."

"That's okay. I'll tell you what to do. I just want you to hold this child while I take about four stitches."

Gwyn felt suddenly dizzy. "S-stitches?"

"Yes. Come on." He went back inside the examining room, where the distraught mother was trying unsuccessfully to comfort her daughter.

Gwyn halted in the doorway. "I don't think I'm any good at this, Doctor."

"There's nothing to it. I'll show you."

"Neal . . ." Her voice took on a pleading tone.

"Look, Gwyn," he said clearly. "I need to take a few stitches. And the mother—" he shook his head "—can't help me. She's too upset and she's transferring that to the little girl. I'm going to ask her to wait outside until I'm finished. You stay here with the child. Her name's Emmy."

Neal pried the upset mother from the child and indicated that Gwyn should take her place. "I'll be right back." Soon he was issuing terse instructions. "Stand here, at her head. I don't have a straitjacket, so you'll have to hold her firmly. But she's little, and I think you can do that with no trouble."

"Straitjacket?"

"You know, it's a contraption to keep little ones from wiggling so you can take stitches or do whatever is necessary for their own good."

"Oh, no, Neal." Gwyn shook her head firmly. "I don't think I can do this. In fact, I know I can't. Furthermore, I don't want to."

"Sure you can. If you don't help me, Gwyn, I can't possibly do it by myself. And this child will heal with a wide scar on her face. Now do you want that?" He looked at her sternly.

Gwyn gazed down at little Emmy's frightened eyes and pretty little face and shook her head. "No."

"Then do as I say. Put your arms alongside her head, like this, and hold her body firmly here. Like this. Good."

Gwyn did as she was told, and Neal draped a sterile cloth around both the child's wound and Gwyn's arms. They were in this thing together, she and little Emmy. Then he turned his back on them, and when he approached again, he held a small syringe and needle.

"Have to anesthetize it," he muttered.

Gwyn gulped and looked away. She had a sinking feeling in the pit of her stomach. *Oh, dear God, what in the world am I doing here?* At that moment she didn't know why she hadn't taken his advice and grabbed a book and stayed away from the clinic.

When Neal touched the child's forehead, she started wriggling and straining against Gwyn's arms. And screaming at the top of her lungs.

"Hold her still," Neal commanded.

Gwyn forgot her own discomfort and her displeasure at having to spend two important weeks in her life in this remote place. Only one thing mattered right now—a little girl named Emmy needed Neal's skills . . . and needed her help.

Gwyn leaned her head close to Emmy's ear and murmured soft, soothing words. As a distraction, she began telling a story about a little girl who'd lost her kitten, complete with the appropriate sounds of the characters.

Suddenly everything was quiet except for Gwyn's voice switching from the imitation of the mewing kitten to the high-pitched little girl. The crying hushed. Emmy was listening.

"Go on with your story," Neal encouraged softly. "It's distracting her."

Gwyn took a deep breath and resumed. She was beginning to understand a tiny speck of Neal's dedication to the people of Harmony Creek. Today she had seen firsthand how badly they needed him and how much he needed help, more than she could give him. Her organization of his office wouldn't improve things dramatically. So what was she doing here? And was there anything she could do? If so, what? More importantly, how?

THAT NIGHT SHE SLUMPED into one of the plump chairs and accepted the cup of hot apple cider Neal handed her. They sipped in absolute silence, each exhausted, each lost in individual thoughts.

Gwyn remembered she hadn't talked to Travis in two days. Two days and a world away. He would scoff at what she'd done today. Basic filing. He would be appalled if she told him her greatest accomplishment was to hold a child still so the doctor could make tiny precise stitches in her forehead. He would be amazed to hear her greatest joy was that Emmy wouldn't grow up with an ugly scar on her beautiful little face.

Neal stared absently at a bubble circling on the surface of his steaming drink. He realized he hadn't been overly receptive to Gwyn. Perhaps it was subconscious. Actually he'd been such a jackass that it was a wonder she hadn't just left Harmony Creek. Was it because her obstinate boss was so demanding? Or because she found two weeks' worth of challenges around here?

He had to admit she'd been a great deal of help today. For someone with no trauma experience, she'd proved herself pretty tough. He should let her know he was grateful.

"Thanks for working on the files. And for helping with Emmy—I realize that must have been hard for you," he offered finally.

"What would you have done if I hadn't been here?"

"If there's no one around the office to help me, I send for Mae or Jed. They live about a mile away through those woods in back of the clinic."

"But that takes time."

"Yes." He nodded slowly.

"And if Mae or Jed aren't available?"

"In this case I'd have closed the laceration with a couple of butterfly Band-Aids and hoped for the best."

"It would help if you had better equipment, wouldn't it?"

He sighed. "Lots of things would help."

"That's what I'm here for, Neal. To try to help you," she said brightly.

"Don't start with that again." His blue eyes were no longer sparkling, but tired and dull.

Gwyn's stomach growled, reminding her she hadn't eaten anything since the cake at noon. "What do you do about dinner around here?"

His gaze traveled to the long table, which was laden with scrumptious treats. "Scrounge. Whatever's here."

"But you haven't had a decent meal today. All those sweets aren't good for you."

"Who's the doc around here?" He looked at her with a glimmer of a teasing twinkle in his eyes.

She smiled in response. "I know something about eating for a healthy body. And coconut cake and berry cobbler won't cut it."

"Can you cook? Help yourself to the kitchen."

She grinned. "I can organize your cupboard shelves in a flash, but cooking isn't my bag. How about if you choose your favorite restaurant? My treat."

He threw back his head and laughed. "Maybe you missed the fact that they roll up the streets of the nearest town at—" he checked his watch "—aw nuts. We just missed the big event."

"Well, I guess it's up to us, then." She sighed heavily, unenthusiastic at the prospect of cooking. "One of my favorite tricks is to mix two different kinds of soup. Got any cans handy?"

"Maybe. I think we have some leftover stew from last night. Put that with something."

"I never promised a gourmet meal, but I'll try to stir up something."

"And I'll knock the chill off the room by starting a fire," he offered.

"Sounds great." Before long Gwyn was puttering around in the kitchen, unaware that she was humming.

Neal whistled while he worked on a fire.

As she filled their bowls, an unusual feeling came over Gwyn. She wanted to please Neal with the soup. Cooking to please had never been a priority of hers. "Hope it's okay."

"I'm sure it is." He nodded toward the fire. "Want to eat over here?"

She agreed and settled near the warm hearth, waiting for his response when he sampled a bite.

"Very good, Gwyn."

"Not great, but better for you than cobbler."

"Maybe so, but just imagine that hot, sweet blackberry juice oozing beneath vanilla ice cream," he taunted.

"Ooh, you're awful! A real sweet junkie."

"You aren't?"

"Not really. I prefer nonsweet junk food like popcorn or chips."

"I'll pop some over the fire tonight."

"Pop it right here?"

"I found a popcorn popper made of wire mesh, probably predates World War II. It was in the bottom of one of the cabinets, forgotten all these years." When they finished their soup, Neal went to the kitchen and pulled out a strange-looking contraption. "See? Put the corn kernels in here and clamp it shut and hold it over the fire. Simple."

She hovered beside him, examining the old utensil. "I've never seen anything like this. Why, it must be an antique."

"Like everything else around here. You know, these old buildings were used as a Civilian Conservation Corps camp during the Depression. The group who stayed here did logging and trail breaking through the mountains. And they left behind their popcorn popper."

"Let's try it out. Got any popcorn?"

"I think it's around here somewhere." He opened one cabinet, then another in his search.

Gwyn tried not to admire Neal's expansive back, long arms and tight, muscular buns as he stretched to see what was on the high shelves. She tried to ignore how very masculine, how appealing, he was to her and wondered if it was because she was lonely tonight.

"Ah, here it is." As he extracted the jar of popcorn from the top shelf, they heard the phone ring. "That's either an emergency for me . . . or your boss checking up on you," he said as he crossed the room to answer it. After a brief exchange he waved the receiver in her direction. "For you."

She hid her disappointment at having to stop their popcorn project and smilingly took the phone. "Hello?"

"Gwyn? Great to hear you made it to the country."

She recognized the familiar voice. "Hello, Travis."

"How's it going?"

"Just fine. There's a lot to be done and not much time to do it."

"Is this the same irate woman who didn't want to waste two weeks on this project?"

She laughed. "Yeah, I guess." Gwyn sat in a ladder-backed chair near the phone. "You wouldn't believe this place, Travis. It took me forever to get here. And the conditions are less than great." She noticed Neal glance up and realized he had heard her comments. Immediately he disappeared behind the door that she assumed led to his bedroom.

"What's the deal?"

"Oh, it's busy. Very busy." She tried to forget about Neal but heard water running and knew he must be taking a shower. The vision of his strong, nude body standing under the flow of steaming hot water flashed through her head. She shook off the image. "How about you, Travis? How are things in the city?"

"I'm going to Milwaukee tomorrow for the rest of the week. It's a busy schedule, including some night meetings, so I might not be able to reach you for a few days. Hang in there. The two weeks will be over before you know it."

Milwaukee, as well as Chicago, seemed a million miles away from Tennessee tonight. "Yeah, sure." Her gaze traveled to a nearby bookshelf, which was loaded with mystery paperbacks, nonfiction books about the

Great Smoky Mountains and medical texts. Tucked
back on one shelf was a frame with holes in the mat-
ting to hold various sizes of photos. "Talk to you later,
Trav."

"I'll call you when I get back."

"Bye." Gwyn hung up the phone and leaned closer
to the photos.

She recognized a young Neal with an older dark-
haired woman. There was a slight resemblance, so she
assumed this was his mother. Next was a snapshot of
Neal and a younger woman holding up fish on a line
and mugging for the camera. Could be a girlfriend. Or
a sister. There were several young men, bare chested
and in jeans, arms slung around shoulders. Then Neal
with a broad, happy grin sitting on the hood of an old
sports car.

In the last photo a nonbearded Neal had his arm
around a beautiful blonde. Instinctively Gwyn knew
she wasn't his sister. Where was she now? And why was
he up here in the mountains, serving rural America's
health needs alone?

Gwyn suddenly realized she felt no regret at being
here for the present. She'd rather be here than in Milwaukee like Travis.

She wandered back to the kitchen, where Neal had
left the antique popcorn popper on the countertop. It
took some doing, but she figured out how it opened and
was holding it over the flames, when he reappeared.

She smiled over her shoulder at him. "I'm trying out
your popcorn popper. Think it works?"

"I know it does. I've used it."

"Would you check and see if I have it closed right?"

He crossed the room and examined the device.
"Looks okay to me."

Gwyn observed his hands, noting the taper of his fingers. She recalled how skillfully they'd made tiny stitches in a small girl's forehead. How gentle yet precise. He smelled of fresh rain in a pine forest, his hair still wet from the shower and slicked back. She thought of running her hands through his clean, damp hair...of his returning the gesture. Her scalp tingled as if with a sudden chill. She shouldn't let herself fantasize about him.

With somewhat shaky hands she took the popcorn popper from him and poked it back over the fire. "How long does it take?"

"Do you gauge everything in time?"

Startled by his abrupt question, she turned her face up to him. "Of course not. I just wondered—" She frowned. "What's wrong? You were perfectly nice all evening, before the phone rang. Almost human. And now—"

"Nothing. It's nothing." He stood back and motioned at the fire. "You have to give the kernels time to get hot. I don't know how long." Why was he behaving like this? It didn't take anything for this woman to get under his skin.

They watched the flames in silence for a full minute.

"I realize my being here has interrupted your lifestyle, Neal," she said finally. "There are probably things you'd rather be doing and people you'd rather be seeing. And I want you to feel free to go ahead."

"No, there's nothing. No one."

"Hey, if we're going to spend two weeks together, maybe it would help if we knew a little something about each other." She kept her gaze on the fire. "The phone call was from my colleague at Mark Time. He used to be my boyfriend." Gwyn hesitated with a little chuckle.

"Sounds silly to call a man who's almost thirty a boy-anything, doesn't it? Now Travis is just a good friend." The first kernel exploded, followed by a series of staccato pops.

Her explanation forgotten for the moment, Gwyn gave Neal an exultant smile. "It works! Look at this! Old-fashioned popcorn!"

Neal watched her enthusiasm grow, as well as the light in her brown eyes. He appreciated the fact that she actually livened up his dull life, and yet he was reacting by being a jerk to her. How stupid! He'd known from the beginning that the phone call hadn't been from her boss. Or from her father. She'd gone out of her way to explain, but what difference did it make? She was here temporarily. At least he could try to make the best of it for both of them.

"Now you," Gwyn prompted.

"Huh?"

"Tell me about you."

"Not much to tell," he muttered stiffly. "Finished my residency at Miami Medical in May. Took this job in June."

"Is that it?" She looked at him with a teasing smile. "No family? No girlfriend?"

"A sister in Fort Lauderdale. That's it."

The popping stopped, and Gwyn pulled the popper from the fire and put it on the hearth. She sat on the chair's edge, hands clutched in her lap. "Then tell me about the people in the photos."

"What photos?"

She motioned. "The ones on the bookshelf."

He shrugged. "Just friends from med school."

"The older lady?"

"My mother. Made about a year before she died."

"I'm sorry." Gwyn felt a pang of sympathy. "And the younger women?

"Sis."

"There are two of them,"

Neal glared at her, his eyes glazed, his mouth slightly agape. He felt a surge of anger. She was intruding. No, she was being normal. People asked questions innocently. What should he say? He'd never explained the situation to anyone, never figured out the right words to make it easier. He simply didn't deal with it. He turned away from Gwyn's expectant face. "She . . ."

Watching his reaction, Gwyn felt a drop in the pit of her stomach. She realized her questions were inappropriate. His reaction was too strong, too abrupt. She tried to soothe her mistake. "You don't have to tell me, Neal."

He finally spoke in a low voice, sounding strained and different. "She died, too . . . a couple . . . of years ago."

"I'm sorry." Gwyn felt terrible and groped for words. "Were you married?"

"No. Engaged."

"I . . . I shouldn't have mentioned it. Didn't mean to bring up bad memories." Gwyn hunkered down in the plump chair like a child who wished to disappear.

"It's okay. You couldn't know." He shook his head. "I'm not very good at dealing with this. Uh, don't mind me. You didn't do anything . . . just forget it, okay?"

"Sure." She felt very uncomfortable and began fiddling with the popcorn popper until it sprang open. "Want some?"

"No, thanks." He studied the fire.

She munched a bite. "Pretty good. Look, Neal, I didn't mean to spoil the evening."

"I know. I'm just . . ."

"Don't...please don't clam up like this, Neal. If you'd rather, I'll just grab one of those books on your shelf, take my popcorn and go to my room. I don't have to be entertained."

He gazed at her for a moment, then his eyes softened. "No, don't do that. I want your company. I...I've been alone too long already. I'm not even behaving decently. To be honest, I haven't tried in a long time." He stared dreamily at the flickering fire. "Do you want some warm blackberry cobbler and ice cream with me?"

She smiled her consent. "Sounds fabulously sinful!"

"It is." He grinned and moved to the kitchen to fix their wicked feast.

Gwyn got a big bowl for the popcorn, and soon they were sitting in front of the fire again, munching and chatting, occasionally laughing. When he chose to, Neal could be extremely nice. But as she'd suspected, those deep, brooding eyes of his hid a mystery.

Suddenly Gwyn was overwhelmed with the urge to solve the mystery of Dr. Neal Perry and to know more about this man who seemed to enjoy a strange and lonely existence hidden away in the Smokies.

3

NEAL PERRY WASN'T LOOKING for a friend. Nor did he need someone to make his life more efficient. He wasn't looking for anything, but instead was running from everything. He knew it and accepted it. And he had found exactly what he wanted in Harmony Creek—a full-time occupation where he could lose himself in his work. Now *she* was here to disrupt his carefully chosen, reclusive life.

He wanted to scorn her for it. But he just couldn't. A thick mane of dark, unruly hair and vibrant brown eyes taunted him, which was unusual. Blondes were more his style. Blondes like Maria.

But Gwyn Frederick wasn't Maria, wasn't anything like her. No one could be.

He fumbled with the coffeepot and found himself trying to be quiet so as not to wake her. His motives had more to do with not wanting to deal with her this morning than with letting her sleep in. She was a pesky type, always checking her list and organizing things. Well, he wouldn't be organized. He liked his life the way it was, spontaneous and unplanned. Neal was confident he could handle most health problems that came through the door. It was enough for him.

Although somewhat aggravating, Gwyn was quite attractive, he'd admit. Her wild curls were the kind men wanted to rake their hands through in a fit of passion, and he'd been tempted a time or two. The color of her eyes reminded him of milk chocolate. When she stopped hounding him about a time schedule and actually smiled, her keen eyes softened considerably. And so did her temperament.

He couldn't help being fascinated with the pouting shape of her lips and the way they seemed to melt into a smile. He'd even wondered, once or twice, about their taste. Beneath that thick, dark hair and contrasting with those snapping, brown eyes was a luscious, golden complexion. He halted and looked down at his knotted fist. What was he doing, letting her occupy his mind like this? What a time waster!

He stepped away from the counter and, with the heels of his hands on the edge of the cabinet, did a few push-ups, then stretched his hamstrings. Flexing his feet, he worked one, then the other. While the coffee sputtered and dripped, he did some side stretching in front of the fireplace, concentrating on his legs and inner thighs. When Gwyn arrived, he was working feverishly on his abdominals.

She had tumbled out of bed early to study her time log from the previous day. Tugging on a warm robe, Gwyn quickly decided she needed a cup of coffee to finish the waking process. So she'd brought her notebook out to the kitchen, thinking she would review her notes quietly until the doctor awoke. She was surprised to find him there already.

Greeted by a regular succession of uncivil sounds, she halted. Then she recognized the grunting as counting. Her gaze swept the room. A warm glow radiated from the low coals, giving the whole place a pink tint. Beyond the fireplace, on a colorful braided rug, stretched Neal's trim figure. He puffed numbers aloud as his upper torso rose for sit-ups.

"Oh. I thought I was the first one up." Gwyn couldn't take her eyes off him.

"Nope." Neal didn't miss a beat.

He wore a cutoff turquoise Miami Dolphins football shirt that hit him midchest. A dark line of hair ran down his torso and disappeared beneath the waistband of loose gray sweatpants. As he labored, the material bunched at his crotch, and Gwyn's imagination accelerated into fifth gear. With his legs bent at the knees and arms folded across his chest, she could appreciate his muscular physique in all its magnificence.

Finally she stuttered an explanation. "I thought I'd just work out . . . er, I mean work *on* a time log for the office. Along with a cup of coffee."

"Help yourself." He didn't stop bending.

"You're sure I won't bother you?" Forcing her gaze away from him, she fumbled with a cup. Of the hundreds of men who worked out at her club, none looked quite this good. She was impressed with the country doctor.

"No more than you already have." As he continued his efforts, a gleam of perspiration spread over his arms and face. "I hope sweat doesn't bother you at this hour of the morning."

"No, not at all." Gwyn laughed nervously and proceeded to pour the coffee she so desperately needed. She had lied. She was very bothered. But it wasn't the man's sweat that disturbed her. It was his *body*. Muscles in all the right places, masculinity in its glory! She could hardly keep her eyes off his enticing, almost erotic form. He was absolutely gorgeous! She thought of the other men she knew...and there was no comparison for raw masculinity.

Gwyn sipped her coffee and opened a folder, staring with glazed, unseeing eyes at the time schedule before her. She listened to his counting and envisioned his body, pumping up and down, up and down. "This is a good way to start the day," she remarked, using idle conversation as an excuse to turn toward him. And watch.

"Exercise—" he panted through two last sit-ups before lying flat "—or coffee?"

"Exercise, of course. I'm surprised you do it."

"Why?"

"Well, for one thing, it's good for you," she admitted tartly. "And you seem intent on testing your body, eating all the wrong stuff and at odd hours."

"So you think I do all the wrong things?"

"Some, not all."

He propped himself up on an elbow and glared at her. "I *am* a doctor, you know. I don't need someone to tell me how to take care of my body."

"I keep reminding myself of that." She shook her head and gestured toward the row of pies and cobblers still waiting to be eaten. "But you consume all this sugar!"

"Exercise makes it possible for me to eat blackberry cobbler for breakfast, lunch and dinner if I want to!" He flipped over and began doing rapid push-ups. He'd show her about testing the body! Who was she to wheel in here and take charge of his office *and* his bad eating habits?

"Yes, exercise does keep the flab off, I suppose," she observed coolly. "For a while. And it's definitely better than doing nothing. It's what all that stuff does to your insides that really matters." She sighed. "Perhaps I should join you. I usually attend an aerobic class after work and haven't exercised in several days now."

"I'm too . . . tired after . . . my work," he muttered.

"I can understand that. I was really bushed last night. You know, maybe it's not such a bad idea to exercise in the mornings."

"You mean . . . you're admitting . . . I do something right? It's a miracle!"

"This is a very good plan, Neal. Mind if I join you tomorrow?"

"I jog tomorrow."

"Jog? That's even better, alternating types of exercises. How far do you go?"

"Coupla miles. Till I feel like quitting."

"What time do you start? I'll set my alarm."

"Time?" He almost growled. "I start when my eyes pop open and the old bod feels like it."

Her temper flared with his sharp answers. "Look, Neal, if you don't want me to join you, just say so."

He finished his push-ups and flopped to his belly, resting his forehead on folded arms. His voice was muffled. "No, I wouldn't consider standing in the way of your workout schedule."

"I can figure my own schedule and work out by myself."

"No, no. Please come along. I can use the company."

"Good." She gave him a satisfied smile, but he wasn't looking. "Maybe we can use the time to go over some of your objectives and priorities."

"Ohhh," he groaned, rolling over. "Don't you ever stop setting time perimeters?"

"That's what I'm here for. To increase efficiency and productivity."

"I thought you were here to help me inoculate babies. And take blood tests." He sat up and twisted back and forth from the waist. "Unfortunately in my ignorance I increased my own productivity."

"I'm working on that, too, Neal," she said confidently.

"How? Are you taking a quick nursing course? Or writing it all down in your log so you can analyze it later?"

She glared at him.

He looked up at her, a teasing light edging into his blue eyes, a small grin starting to form. "Sorry. All this organization talk bugs me. So much of my life is geared to spontaneity and taking care of a problem as it appears that it seems a waste to try to organize it."

"But don't you see how preplanning can avoid some crises before they happen?"

"When it comes to illnesses and accidents, planning flies out the window. And I have to deal immediately with real people."

"I'd like to help."

"Whatever." He sighed and leaped to his feet. "Now, my stomach calls for breakfast. I think it's saying banana pudding today." He paused beside the table, dabbed his finger in one Pyrex dish and sensuously licked it clean. "Hmm, Myrtle's pudding is out of this world! And coffee goes perfectly with pudding, so that's next on my list. Then my sweaty body dictates that I take a shower and get dressed for work. See how common sense takes the place of a list? No offense to your job or anything, Gwyn."

"Of course not." She scoffed at him and shook her head with a good-natured smile.

He poured a cup of coffee, piled a bowl full of pudding and headed for the door to his room. "You don't mind if I'm not exactly sociable this a.m., do you? My inner clock says for me to get a move on."

"That goes for both of us." She chuckled and tried to sound nonchalant, in spite of her wild mixture of feelings when he left the room.

A moment later he poked his head back through the door. "Forgive my sadly lacking Southern hospitality. Please help yourself to breakfast. There's cereal.... No, it's sugar coated. Well, there're eggs.... No, too much cholesterol." He shrugged and pointed to the table, laden with dessert treasures. "There's always..."

"Do you have any fresh fruit?"

"In the pie. Try Adalie's blackberry cobbler. She wins the blue ribbon at the fair every year!"

Gwyn gaped at him for a moment, then broke into laughter. "Okay. I think I'm being corrupted!"

"Didn't they ever teach you if you can't beat 'em, compromise?"

"Yes." She stretched the word out slowly. "Does that serve for us, too?"

"Actually I was going to declare a truce today. You do your thing. And I'll do mine."

And never the twain shall meet, she thought. She felt rebuffed. "Truce it is, then. And I promise to stay out of your way, Doctor."

"Great." He answered fast and disappeared again.

This time he didn't return. And Gwyn knew she had her work, and hopes of any peaceful relationship with this man, cut out for her.

Their self-imposed truce lasted the day, and by evening both were too tired to spar. Gwyn had dedicated herself to finishing the files that day. She found that he had a system, although it was slow and outdated. Nothing a computer system wouldn't fix. But that, under the present circumstances, was an impossibility. She continued to meet patients, discuss payment options with them and make several appointments for follow-ups.

Neal had been content to take care of the steady stream of patients. Many were families with more than one child who needed and received inoculations. As a result, the day was filled with crying children. Gwyn was almost ready to scream by nightfall, and Neal was exhausted. They ate a macaroni salad in almost total silence. Neal didn't even notice that one of his patients had brought it. And that it wasn't some sweet concoction. But Gwyn did. And she was privately satisfied. Her plan was working.

THE NEXT MORNING she was ready and waiting when Neal entered the kitchen dressed in gray sweats. With his dark hair and beard, he looked devastating in gray! His blue eyes were hooded and marvelously sexy. Gwyn wrenched her gaze away from his appealing physical build and pretended to be interested in doing a runner's stretch.

"Morning," he mumbled, reaching for a glass of juice.

"Good morning," she said, sounding much more chipper than he.

He looked glumly at her, dressed in her snappy little red velour jogging suit. She was bright and cheerful, a welcome change from the solemn way he usually greeted the morning. Maybe he'd been tucked away too long, growing mellow and staying angry with the world. "Ready to jog?"

She nodded eagerly. "You have an early appointment, so we'd better be going."

"Appointment?"

"Mrs. Nelson is bringing some of the kids in for their shots before school starts. She works, too, so it's more convenient for everyone."

"Everyone?" He looked at her accusingly.

"Yes." Gwyn lifted her chin defiantly. "That's what a schedule does. It molds to accommodate everyone's time. Otherwise, she'd have to bring in four children, and they'd all have to sit in your office until you could get to them. The kids would miss school, and Mrs. Nelson would miss work. With an appointment, they can see the doctor with little interruption to their lives."

He folded his arms. "And the doctor?"

"Better for you, too. You take care of the Nelson family in one trip, giving them quality, uninterrupted attention. And by allowing Mrs. Nelson to go on to work on time, she won't have to take a financial cut and will be in better shape to pay you eventually." She folded her arms to match his position.

"Mrs. Nelson works in her family's company, Nelson Gravel. I doubt they'll dock her pay."

"I give up!" Gwyn raised her hands in a frustrated gesture. "You are amazingly stuck in your ways for a young man."

Neal nodded. "Yep, I guess I am. But experience does that to you." He led the way outside and into the woods behind the clinic.

Gwyn followed, trying to match her speed with his naturally rhythmic, long-legged stride. The earth was damp and cool in the early-morning hours. But it felt good to breathe deeply and run. When the path widened, she jogged beside him. "I don't know what happens when I start to work, Neal. Maybe it's just that I see so much that needs to be done around here that I want to renovate everything. I really don't intend to interfere with your way of doing things."

"I know what you're trying to do, Gwyn. In theory and in city businesses it works. But out here it's different. I keep thinking that after you leave, I'll be alone again. And who'll get the phone and keep up the schedules you set into motion?"

"I'm aware of that. And it's one of my concerns," she admitted. "I'm trying to figure a remedy."

"The remedy is to hire office help," he said firmly.

"Then why doesn't the Rural Health Service do that?" It sounded logical to her.

"The pay is low. Biggest problem . . ." He was panting now. "Nobody wants to come to such an outpost."

"But they found a doctor. Why did you come here?"

"I'd just finished my trauma and emergency care residency and was willing to accept the remoteness. Most nurses can get a better job than this in a city hospital with much better conditions and benefits.

Gwyn was aware that he hadn't really answered her question about him. Obviously he felt the real reason he'd come here was none of her business. "So there is a salary allowance available through the federally funded Rural Health Service? It's just a matter of finding someone to fill the position?"

"As I said, it's not that easy."

"How did they find you?"

"Advertised in the *Miami Herald*."

"And you knew you wanted this kind of job? Even with the drawbacks, you applied anyway?"

"Yep." He followed a right fork in the path. "Here's another of your textbook theories. Problem stated, obstacles faced, solution figured, now make it work."

"Neal, you don't know me very well," Gwyn said. "I'm very tenacious. I'll find a way to make it work."

"I could figure that much." He glanced over at her. "Another of your plans to leave this a better place?"

"Part of the plan," she confirmed with a smile.

They continued running, both breathing hard now, until eventually they reached a clearing and a neat little farmhouse.

"This is where Mae and Jed McPherson live," Neal said, bounding onto the front porch. He knocked on the door, but no one answered. "Too bad they aren't here. I wanted you to meet Mae. Jed is the one who picked you up in town the other night."

"Oh, yes. And Mae's the one who sent the stew we ate when I arrived."

Neal hopped off the porch. "Mae's an amazing woman. She drives a two-ton dump truck for Nelson Gravel Company."

"Talk about your liberated women!" Gwyn laughed and followed Neal around the farmhouse, where they picked up the trail through the woods again. On the trip back Gwyn reflected that Neal could be friendly, even nice. It was possible for them to get along, for she'd seen signs here and there. Like now. He couldn't be more amiable. So why wasn't he this way all the time?

At any rate, she was glad she'd set her alarm and come jogging with him. He'd given her insight into solving some of the logistical problems around the clinic. But what piqued her curiosity the most was strictly personal. Why had the young Dr. Perry, just finishing his residency, been willing to take such an outpost as Harmony Creek?

When they arrived back at the clinic, the Nelson family was already waiting on the front porch. "They're early," Gwyn moaned.

"There goes the plan to shower before I start," Neal answered under his breath.

Gwyn continued with him. "I set this up, so I'll help."

"Inoculate? My, my, you're a fast study."

She tightened her lips. "I'll get their files for you."

"Actually this shouldn't take long. Maybe we can still shower after the shots and before the rush."

The minute the Nelson's four-year-old took one look at Neal, he started wailing. That upset the baby, who also started to cry. The other two, who according to the chart were six and seven, clung to their mother's shirttail. Mrs. Nelson tried to calm her children and talk sensibly to Neal at the same time. The whole scene quickly became chaotic, for in the midst of the cacophony, Mae and Jed McPherson arrived.

"Jed cut his hand. It's bad," Mae announced. "Clear the way." She elbowed a path through the assemblage of crying and clinging children, while Jed followed.

"What happened?" Neal directed the question to Jed.

"It's not too bad, Doc—" he began.

Mae interrupted loudly. "Why he dang near cut his whole hand off!"

Everyone gasped and craned to see the crudely wrapped hand of Jed McPherson. Neal directed him to one of the examining rooms.

"Mae got a little scared, Doc, that's all…." Jed shook his head and disappeared, along with Mae and Neal.

Miraculously there was a moment of peace and quiet because the children stopped their crying when the doctor disappeared from sight. Gwyn sighed with relief and smiled weakly at Mrs. Nelson. "Just have a seat and the doctor will be with you as soon as he takes care of this emergency."

Mrs. Nelson approached the desk, an uneasy expression on her face. "I need to talk to someone about paying our bill. We still owe from when Ozzie, the four-year-old, was sick with tonsillitis three months ago. And now all these shots—"

The examining room door opened and Neal barked, "Gwyn!"

Then Mae appeared, ashen faced, and leaned against the wall.

"Excuse me, Mrs. Nelson. We'll discuss this in a few minutes." Gwyn hurried to Mae's side. "Are you all right? Come over here and have a seat."

Mae obliged, and Gwyn brought her a glass of cold water. "I don't know what happened to me. I've never fainted in my life." She gave an embarrassed little laugh. "But when the doctor started getting ready to take stitches in Jed's hand, I felt dizzy all of a sudden."

Gwyn placed a wet paper towel on her forehead and reassured her everything would be all right.

In a few minutes Mae looked up at Gwyn and smiled. "Thanks for your help. You must be Doc's new nurse."

"Well, actually I...I'm here to help in the office." She decided that now wasn't the time to explain. "I'm Gwyn Frederick. And you must be Mrs. McPherson. I've heard many good things about you."

"Call me Mae," the gray-haired lady said with a shrug. "Everybody else does. We've all been waiting anxiously on you, Missy. Especially the doc."

Gwyn's heart sank. Waiting anxiously? No wonder Neal was so disappointed when he discovered she wasn't a nurse. His expectations were so completely different from what she could deliver. "I want to thank you, Mae, for the stew you sent over. It was delicious. Nutritious, too. I'm afraid too many of the ladies in the community are sending sweets to the doctor. You should see the stack of pies he has."

"Well, you don't have to worry about me fixing him any pies. Stew is my best dish." She chuckled. "I'm not much of a cook."

"You know, in a barter system people usually exchange what they need, can use or would buy anyway. I wish I could convince people around here that Dr. Perry doesn't need all those sweets. But there are other things he could use. I'd like to coordinate those needs with available products or services."

"You're a good nurse, wanting to take care of the doctor like that." Mae patted Gwyn's hand.

Gwyn cleared her throat. She probably shouldn't let the mistaken identity continue, but now seemed an inappropriate time to explain that she was an organizer, not a nurse. "Neal, er, Dr. Perry tells me you drive a dump truck."

"Only part-time."

"Still, that's quite a tough job."

"Maybe so. But I wasn't very tough in there, was I?" She pointed toward the closed door that hid Jed and Neal.

"I think your reaction was a perfectly normal one," Gwyn said gently.

"You're nice." Suddenly Mae gazed up at Gwyn with a little smile. "Excuse me for asking, but are you married?"

"No, but I—"

"Have a boyfriend," Mae finished. "Of course you do. A pretty girl like you would, I suppose. Still, the doctor is a handsome man, don't you think so?"

"Yes."

"He's very smart and a good man. He'll make someone a good catch someday."

"I'm sure."

"We're really lucky to have him here in Harmony
Creek," Mae continued.

"Yes, I agree."

"We need him so badly. But he has needs, too." Mae
lowered her voice and leaned toward Gwyn. "He's a
lonely man, that doctor."

Gwyn groped for words. "Well, he has a dedicated
life."

Mae rocked forward with a slow nod. "Lonely and
sad."

At that moment the examining room door opened,
and Gwyn sighed with relief.

Jed emerged with a freshly bandaged hand and a reassuring smile for his wife. "The doc fixed me right up.
Almost as good as new."

Gwyn met Neal's gaze for a moment, her brown eyes
soft and smiling. She couldn't help the feelings of awe
and admiration that swelled in her breast when she was
presented with continued evidence of his capable heal-
ing abilities. He was remarkable.

But Neal quickly turned away from her, his expression serious, his attention on his next patients. The two
youngest Nelsons started to cry again.

It was noon before Neal and Gwyn managed to
change from their sweats. Even then they had to take
turns so someone could remain in the busy office.
Gwyn went first while Neal was finishing the last patient. Standing under the welcome, warm shower, she
thought of Mae's comments about the lonesome, sad

doctor of Harmony Creek. They only fueled more curiosity about the man Neal Perry.

She hurried back and found Neal in the tiny lab. "Your turn. I made coffee."

"Good. That'll keep us going for the rest of the day." He adjusted a slide under the microscope. "Along with the blackberry cobbler."

"You should eat that macaroni salad. It's better for you."

He looked up, immediately irritated by her directive on what he should eat. Then he caught a whiff of her delicious scent, a luscious spiced-honey fragrance, and his inner messages became jumbled. He was inexorably drawn to her as a man to a beautiful woman, yet something in him raged over her attempts at a smooth dictatorial takeover of his office as well as his personal life.

Her hair, still damp from the shower, framed her fresh-scrubbed face in dark twists. She hadn't bothered with much makeup, and her natural beauty grabbed his aesthetic sense and shook it until he privately acknowledged she was a lovely woman to whom he was unavoidably attracted. But he couldn't let himself be so weak. Not now. He wasn't ready. His response was sharp. "You eat the macaroni. I want the cobbler."

"But you ate banana pudding for breakfast."

"It has eggs."

"And sugar! I give up!" Gwyn turned her face heavenward and gestured in frustration. Then she looked back at him seriously. "No, I can't give up. This is too important."

He shook his head. "Why do I feel as though I'm talking to my mother?"

She folded her arms. "Because you're talking to someone who cares."

Neal could think of no retort. And there was a moment of silence when neither could do a thing but stare at the other.

Then Gwyn managed to stammer, "What I mean is, I . . . I care about the doctor who has such an awesome responsibility to all these people. To your patients. You must know I'm right about what's best for you."

"*I* know what's best for me." He gestured to his heart. "So why don't you let me take care of me, and you take care of the schedule?"

"Is that the way you want it?"

A muscle in his jaw flexed. "Yes, I do."

She raised her chin. "Okay, Mr. Sweet-slob, go for it! But when you develop some awful disease of the blood and arteries, don't forget that someone warned you once upon a time!" She wheeled around, flushed with conflicting emotion. When she felt his hand on her arm, she stopped.

"Gwyn, hold it." His voice was low and apologetic. "I'm . . . sorry. You're absolutely right. I'm a food slob. And I needed someone like you to point it out. I've known it all along. Don't know why I'm resisting the truth." He knew why. He was resisting *her*.

She turned around slowly, his hand still on her arm, her heart pounding. She gazed at him, a puzzled expression in her eyes. "You waste valuable time ridiculing and countering my attempts to improve your situation around here. Then, when you have a minute to think, you reverse your opinion and apologize. I don't understand you, Neal."

"It isn't necessary for you to understand." He stiffened and presented his enigmatic facade again, protecting and hiding. "I'd like you to know, though, that I appreciate your work. If you hadn't been here to keep people flowing through this office, I'd have been in a big mess."

"I'm glad I could help." She looked down at his hand, still on her arm. "And that you can see it."

"They have a saying around here." He grinned and, whether he realized it or not, let his keep-out facade slip a little. "Without you, I'd be up the creek without a paddle. Don't think I'm not aware of how much you're doing. I'm grateful you're here, Gwyn."

"You sure have a strange way of showing it."

"I know." He pressed his lips together and released her arm. There'd be no apology for that. It was just his way. She'd have to accept it. "I'll finish with this patient and take a break to shower and change, if you'll keep a lid on the office." He paused. "And I'll eat the macaroni salad."

She smiled and a tiny flicker lit her brown eyes. Maybe something was working. "Would you mind if I borrow your car to go to the store later? We could use some fresh fruit and vegetables."

"Fine with me. It's a stick-shift Jeep. Keys are in the top drawer of the dresser in my bedroom. Help yourself."

"Thanks." She smiled as he left her side. The man was moody, arrogant and only occasionally nice. Why was she so taken with him that her heart was still pounding? Was he *really* glad she was there? She only knew she was glad to be in Harmony Creek, to have had the opportunity to meet someone like this country doctor who was so dedicated he ignored his own needs. Mae had said he was lonely.

Gwyn wanted more than ever to make this a better place when she left. And, for some crazy reason, she wished she could do something about Neal's loneliness. She couldn't help thinking it had to do with the blonde in the photo. The one who had died. And if that was the case, it was none of Gwyn's business. She should stay out of Neal's personal affairs.

But Gwyn's heart pounded a different message about the man. She realized from the start that he attracted her in many ways. Unfortunately she must have the opposite effect on him.

4

"OKAY, it doesn't always work."

"Theories are like that."

"Time management planning isn't a theory. It's been proved effective in all aspects of life, both business and personal."

"Not here. We deal with human needs and crises." Neal was preparing the coffeepot the next morning as he spoke.

"But that doesn't mean you have to function on a crisis level at all times." Gwyn inserted an exercise tape in her portable radio. "If you do, you'll have no time for planning."

"Oh, I'm really concerned about that." Neal leaned his hips against the kitchen counter and watched her through still-sleepy eyes. She was certainly enough to wake a guy up fast in her bright pink tights and black leotard cut high on the hips.

That darned outfit made her long, slender legs look even longer. His familiarity with the human body and its natural imperfections gave Neal a greater appreciation of the merits of hers. With a tiny smile of approval he viewed her from a man's perspective and decided that her curves were shaped quite artistically. And, as most good art, watching her was extremely pleasing to the eye.

Gwyn continued with her favorite subject, oblivious to his mesmerized gaping. "The definition of crisis is 'something unexpected that changes the course of events.' The purpose of planning is to reduce the chances of those crises, not necessarily to eliminate them. You anticipate, prevent and limit." She looked up, suddenly aware of his gaze on her. "What's wrong?"

"Not a thing." He smiled and motioned with one hand. "Go on."

She began to stretch slowly from her waist. "I have an old saying for you. If you're always up to your neck in alligators, when do you have time for your real objective of draining the swamp?"

He watched her graceful, sensuous movements and decided she gave new meaning to the phrase "physically fit." "All I do is fight the alligators. I'm not out to change the world, just cure my little corner of it."

She straightened and put her hands on her hips. "And I'm not out to organize it. But while you're so busy fighting your alligators, you aren't leaving any time for yourself, Neal. And that's important, too. Because someday you'll break down, and the fight will be lost. The alligators will take over."

"And you think organizing will prevent such a disaster?" He, too, began to stretch.

"I know it will." She flipped on the tape, and a woman's sonorous voice began instructions on proper stretching methods. Gwyn bent from the waist, twisting and turning slowly in time with the contemporary tune.

Neal was amused...and impressed. "I don't think I've ever done this to music."

"It's better this way. Adds rhythm and diversion to the routine, boring chore." She touched alternate toes and grinned up at him between her wide-spread legs.

He shrugged and followed suit. Who could deny that musical exercise had worked wonders on her body?

"I've been thinking, Neal."

"Oh, no. Not again."

She ignored his verbal jab and continued her methodical stretching of every major muscle group from neck to toes. "What you need to do is schedule a regular lunchtime. And keep it consistent."

"Is that anything like the appointments you made for yesterday morning?" He proceeded to do everything she did, in his own awkward fashion.

"The schedule was interrupted by a crisis, Neal. That'll happen from time to time and will just have to be handled as it occurs."

"Thanks for letting me take care of my patients."

"If you schedule a set lunchtime, your patients will learn—"

"Not to get sick then?"

She paused long enough to fling him a chiding glance. "They'll know the doctor will always be out from twelve to one."

"That's too long. Doesn't take me an hour to eat."

"Not to gulp down some dessert. To eat something decent, you need more time. Then maybe you'd want to relax with some music or... whatever *you* want to do."

"Maybe I could run into town for a quick movie," he quipped.

"Neal, I'm serious. When a person is as busy as you are, you need to schedule time for yourself, recreational time, as well as work time. It's very important." She moved skillfully from an upper body stretch into a runner's stretch. "If you feel that an hour's too long, make it at least forty-five minutes. But the most important thing is to make it regular."

He mimicked her actions as one stretch led into another, but his movements were ungainly compared to hers. "I'll take your suggestions into consideration."

"That's all I ask." The tempo of the music changed to a more upbeat sound, and she smiled broadly. "Ready for aerobics?" Gwyn raised her arms high, leading the energetic bouncing until they were both puffing. After a cool down she motioned to the quilt she'd spread on the floor. She positioned herself carefully on one side. "Don't stop now. This is for firm inner thighs. Hips aligned, upper leg crossed to brace, lift lower leg just this much. Concentrate on this particular muscle." She pointed to it, then began lifting her leg in time to the beat. "One-two, three-four . . ."

Neal did it, too. But he was having a devil of a time thinking about his own inner thigh muscle. It was much more interesting to concentrate on hers.

They worked on outer thighs and abdominals, then Neal did push-ups while Gwyn did kneeling leg lifts. He couldn't resist watching her with sideways glances. Her legs were gorgeous and her body toned and firm. If she did this regularly, he could see why she looked so good. She worked hard at exercising, just as she worked hard at everything else. "You're very good at this," he said, slumping to the floor when he finished push-ups.

"We aren't done yet. We need to do some final stretching." When he complied, she grinned. "Do you realize this is the first time you've been agreeable about anything I've done around here? Now how am I going to tell my boss that the best thing I did at the clinic was to give a good workout?"

"Sounds like a good day's work to me." He turned on his side and watched her finish some pelvic tilts. Talk about sexy! He had to do some quick mental gymnastics to prevent his own physical response.

"That's not what I'm here for," she countered.

"Look, I know you mean well with your scheduling, Gwyn. It's just that to be hemmed in with a set time for everything goes against my nature. I'll admit, though, you've done a great job of getting the filing system up-to-date and orderly."

"Supplies are next. That system is a disaster."

"I'm impressed with your ambition. Supplies are always a headache."

She sat across from him, legs folded Indian-style. "I intend to conquer that if it kills me. And to leave you with an easier method for reordering when products are low."

"Good. You're making me regret all those nasty little thoughts I had when I discovered you weren't a nurse."

"Now that I see how badly you need one, I understand." She leaned forward to stretch her back. "You're forgiven."

"Did I apologize?"

She frowned at him. "You'd better."

He laughed and tried to do what she was doing. Grunting with the strain, he muttered, "You're doing great. And I appreciate it." He meant more than office work.

"Thanks. That means a lot. Now I can report to my boss that the doctor approves of organization—he just doesn't like doing it." She bent her legs and leaned backward and stretched her upper thighs. "That reminds me. I received a call in the office yesterday from a Representative Sanders. He's bringing some members of the media from Chattanooga tomorrow to interview us about the SHARE program and what it's doing for the rural medical program."

Neal sat upright and squinted at her. "What?"

"I figured you wouldn't mind."

"I don't really care. It's just that I don't see any benefit in it. Talk about your time wasters."

"Well, apparently Representative Sanders thinks it's important. He wants to make it an item. You know how politicians are." She slapped her thighs and jiggled them to loosen the tight muscles.

Neal pushed himself to his knees, then stood with a groan. "Why not?"

They'd practically finished when they heard a large truck engine out front. Then, above the music, the ear-piercing squeak of wheel brakes followed by the whoosh of air brakes, the clanking of metal against metal, the groan of gears shifting.

"What the heck is that?" Neal started to peer out the front window, when a prolonged extremely loud hiss resounded against the walls of the old building, shaking them with the audio vibrations. He headed for the door, instead.

Gwyn clicked the tape player off and rushed after him. "Must be the gravel," she said.

He reached for the doorknob and halted midstep to look back at her. "What did you say?"

"Gravel. The Nelsons wanted to contribute something and suggested their own product, gravel. I agreed. The parking lot is a mess, and I understand it gets worse with the winter rains. This will be so nice. It'll help everyone." She gave him a weak smile. "It will be fine, won't it?"

"Yeah, just fine." He shook his head. "I never know what to expect from you, Gwyn. You're full of surprises."

"This isn't from me. Anyway, surprises keep you on your toes."

"Or in crisis."

"This isn't a crisis. It was planned."

"I just wish I knew your plans."

"Actually this was Mrs. Nelson's idea. She and Mae worked it out and called me."

"Any other calls yesterday that I should know about?"

Gwyn shook her head cheerfully and pushed gently on his arm. "Let's go see."

He stepped outside and, with Gwyn beside him, watched in awe as the giant dump truck inched forward, slowly releasing its full load of gravel in the parking lot. When the job was complete, the driver maneuvered the huge vehicle to a stop near the clinic and hopped out.

"Mae!" Gwyn exclaimed at the gray-haired woman who approached them.

"Here you go, Doc. This place's gonna look like new in a few hours," Mae said with a smile. "Howdy-do, Gwyn."

"Mae, what's going on here?" Neal motioned to the parking lot.

"Can't you see? It's gravel for this mud lot of yours. We wanted to dump it before more rains set in. I checked with your nurse yesterday, and she said it would be fine. Better than more pie!"

"My nurse?"

"Well, you see—" Gwyn began, knowing she should have explained earlier.

"My, my, Missy," Mae interrupted, giving Gwyn an elaborate once-over in her skin-hugging tights and leotard. "You sure are a skinny little thing. How about if you and the good doctor come over to our house tomorrow night for supper? I'll see if I can fatten you up a bit."

Gwyn turned a sweet smile toward Mae. "Well, I . . . that sounds wonderful. If the *good doctor* doesn't have other plans."

Neal cast Gwyn a sideways glance. "If *my nurse* agrees, we'd love to, Mae."

"It might be beef stew again."

"You know it's my favorite." Neal waved toward the gravel. "Now, are you going to explain this, Mae?"

"Mr. Nelson . . . well to be honest, it was Mrs. Nelson who sent it. And I volunteered to dump it. You give us all so much, Dr. Perry, that we wanted to give you something back. So here it is. Now, I've gotta hurry back to work. I'm taking Jed's place full-time until his hand heals."

"How's he feeling?"

"Spent a restless night. Stubborn fool wouldn't take that medicine you sent him until two in the morning. Didn't want to take any drugs. But I convinced him it was different, being prescribed by the doctor. After that, he slept like a baby."

Neal grinned. "I should have ordered a shot of bourbon, instead. He wouldn't have refused that. No bleeding or throbbing?"

"I think he's going to be fine, Doctor. Why, he's already complaining about not being able to work. Complaining's a good sign I always say."

"Me, too," Gwyn agreed with a sly glance at Neal.

"Don't worry about this mess, Doctor. Clyde Nelson is bringing his oldest son over to finish spreading it in a little while."

"This is going to be great. I can't thank you enough, Mae." Neal took her hand.

She smiled up at him, her gently wrinkled face aglow with admiration for the man. "Just keep being our doctor. That's all we want. See you two tomorrow night." Waving, she climbed into the giant truck's cab and drove away as if she were wheeling a compact car.

Before Gwyn and Neal had time to return to their workout, Clyde and his son, Kane, a boy of about fourteen, arrived with equipment to spread the gravel. After exchanging greetings and introductions, the two started to work, and Neal and Gwyn went back inside.

"Looks like we're out of time." She unplugged the radio and wound the cord around it. "Why don't you take the first shower?"

He gaped at her, hands on his hips. "You're telling people that you're my nurse?"

"No, well, you see, that was Mae's mistake. She thought I was a nurse when Jed was injured, and she was so upset I just didn't have the heart to tell her then. I should have, I suppose." Gwyn shrugged apologetically. "But I could see how much she needed a nurse right then. And I couldn't disappoint her. I'll set the record straight. Soon."

"Like tomorrow night?"

"Yes. I will when we go over for dinner. Sorry if I embarrassed you, Neal."

He ran his hand around the back of his neck. "I don't know, Gwyn. I feel as if I'm out of control around here. You're taking charge.'"

"Oh, no, you aren't. My whole purpose is to help you get control of your time and your life." She smiled reassuringly. "And you're on your way. Aren't you pleased with what your patients are doing for the clinic? It was all their idea."

"All, Gwyn?"

"Yes. Mae called me with the plan. She just wanted to know what time would be convenient."

"You didn't suggest anything? Like not to bring desserts around here? Or to dump gravel instead of pies?"

"Well . . ." She toyed with a loose string on her leotard. "I did say there were other ways they could contribute besides bringing sweets."

"Gwyn, this could be another crisis! I might not get any more of Adalie's blackberry cobbler! Or Myrtle's banana pudding! And I happen to like them—No, I *love* them!"

"Nonsense. As soon as I leave, there'll be a string of women at your door with their best desserts." She grinned. "My only hope is that I've had some impact on you by then. And you'll have the willpower to resist."

"Never!" He walked to the coffeepot and poured two cups of black coffee, handing her one. "Oh, you've had an impact, all right. No sugar and cream, see?"

"Persistence works." Grinning, she sipped the strong black brew. "You're very important, Neal. Especially to these people in Harmony Creek. And as I get to know you, I understand why. You're very special to them. You should take care of yourself."

Suddenly she wanted to tell him that he was special to her, too. And yet she couldn't. Shouldn't! Why, how could this man she barely knew be special to her? She was here to do a job. She'd be leaving in a little more than a week.

"You're quite persuasive, Gwyn," Neal said, his tone suddenly soft. Then, snapping himself out of the tender moment, he slapped his hands together. "Well, I'd better change, or I'll be practicing medicine in my sweats again."

"Me, too." She took a deep breath and another sip of coffee. "Sweats aren't exactly my professional attire, either."

He looked pointedly at her. "Out here, though, you can see that it doesn't matter. When someone needs you, it doesn't matter what you wear or what your schedule is."

Gwyn nodded and gathered her portable radio under one arm as she headed for her room. She couldn't get over her mixture of feelings. She was undeniably, strongly attracted to the doctor, to this very special man. Plus she was struck with the realization that she hadn't thought of home all week.

AT LUNCHTIME the clock sign on the office door indicated the doctor would be out until one. Inside the kitchen Neal enjoyed a tuna sandwich at the table and read a week-old newspaper. Gwyn curled up on the sofa with a fashion magazine, munching her tuna on a bed of lettuce. The radio was low, the music mellow, the atmosphere serene. No one spoke or cried or made any demands. Neal thought it was like heaven. Almost.

He glanced at Gwyn, unable to forget the sight of her with those bright pink legs and her shapely body in that black leotard. Actual heaven would be taking her in his arms. Heaven would be holding her and . . . He forced his eyes back to the newspaper. What was wrong with him, anyway? One attractive woman came into his life and he developed a lust for her that kept him awake nights.

But this one was different. She cared about him. He took a deep breath. That was even worse. Maria had cared about him, too, and see what had happened? Why did he have to keep thinking of Maria? Did everyone have to be compared with her? Unfortunately he knew that answer. And until he stopped comparing everyone with her, he couldn't get on with his life. Until he met Gwyn he hadn't even wanted to.

But now, for reasons he couldn't pinpoint, he did. He wanted to live and laugh again. Wanted to participate in the real world, maybe even to love again. *Maybe.* He glanced at Gwyn. She had straightened her legs, flexing her toes, her low-heeled shoes abandoned on the floor. She looked up, caught him staring and smiled.

"Isn't this nice?" she asked, fully expecting his agreement.

He didn't disappoint her. "Mmm-hmm, sure. Just great."

"When I make my weekly report to my boss, I can say I taught the doctor to schedule a lunch break." She grinned teasingly. "He won't understand the magnitude of this accomplishment, though."

"But you do."

"Yes."

"That's all that counts, then." Neal turned back to his newspaper. If he had his way, he'd close the office for the afternoon, grab Gwyn's hand and run off to the woods with her. And that was absolutely crazy! Then he said something equally crazy, without any forethought or analysis of the repercussions. "Would you like to go to a movie tonight?"

Gwyn blinked, not sure she'd heard him right. "Pardon?"

"If you'd like to get out of here and do something different, we could see a movie tonight. Murphy is a little town about twenty miles away, across the North Carolina border. It has a theater that usually gets movies within, oh, two or three years of their release, so it probably wouldn't be anything very current, but . . ."

"You don't have to convince me to go to a movie, Neal." She smiled gently. "I'd love to." She was so pleased he'd suggested going out that she didn't even ask what was showing. It didn't matter.

"We could even have dinner before the show. I hear there are a couple of pretty good restaurants in town."

"Great." She looked back down at the magazine, but nothing registered. Nothing except the fact that Neal had asked her out. It was probably a casual, meaningless gesture, a diversion from the boredom of having her here all the time. Or maybe it was something else. A date? No, that's silly, she thought. But her heart pounded with great expectation.

The afternoon fairly flew by, and Neal couldn't figure why. Maybe it was the improved quality of lunch. He had to admit he felt better and had more energy. Maybe it was the specific routine of exercises Gwyn had conducted that morning. Or maybe it was his outright anticipation of spending an evening out with her. The idea sounded more like a date than just something different to do. And he hadn't had a date, a real date where two people did something entertaining other than sex, in almost two years. It had been almost two years.

No! He wouldn't think of her. Wouldn't let Maria's memory interfere with this evening. It wasn't fair to Gwyn. Nor to him. He had to think of the present now.

Gwyn spent the afternoon in anticipation of the evening, too. While she made diligent lists of supplies and struggled over the difficult and unfamiliar medical terminology, she envisioned riding off that night next to Neal. As she typed everything on a form she'd made specifically for this purpose, she imagined sitting close to him in a movie. Maybe holding hands—No, this was crazy! Absolutely juvenile. She wouldn't think about that. But she couldn't help herself.

THE EVENING STARTED OUT slowly, with brief snatches of conversation interspersed with silence during the drive to Murphy. The quaint little town fairly glowed with Christmas cheer, and the warm spirit of the season seemed to permeate the evening. Neal swept his arm around her as they walked down the sidewalk to the restaurant. It was just a casual motion, Gwyn told herself.

Later as they strolled hand in hand to the theater, Gwyn tried to calm down, but her heart wouldn't listen. She'd seen the movie the year before but wouldn't spoil tonight's fun by admitting it. *Moonstruck* was never like this, however. Being with Neal occupied her total consciousness.

The figures blurred on the screen as she became aware that he had tucked her arm under his and was clasping her palm in his. Their hands rested naturally on one of his thighs, an innocent but intimate act that made keeping her mind on the movie difficult. Impossible, actually!

By the time they were heading home, they had no conversation lag. They talked about the movie, which led to a discussion of their own families.

"I'm surrounded by relatives in and around Chicago," Gwyn revealed. "My father has five brothers and sisters and they all had kids. Now those kids have kids—" She halted and laughed. "There seems to be no end!"

"They have to follow tradition," Neal said with a grin.

"Or something like that." Gwyn shook her head, remembering some of the Frederick family fiascos. "I didn't even mention my mother's three sisters and their families. Some are not on speaking terms, but I won't go into that now."

"You could really relate to that movie, then, couldn't you?"

"We aren't Italian, but, yes, there are similarities. Now, my parents had only three kids, so you might say they broke tradition with big families. My brother, Bob, is married to Celeste, and they have three kids. My younger sister, Angie, has been married to Andrew for about six months." She gazed at Neal's profile in the darkness of the Jeep. "You don't have a big family, I take it?"

"No." He pursed his lips for a few moments before revealing what must have been a rather painful family saga. "My father took off soon after my little sis was born, so my mother raised two kids alone. She never remarried. I suspect she didn't really trust men after that. She died five years ago, and my sis married soon after that. So it's just the two of us."

"You never married?"

"No." He gazed straight ahead. "You?"

"Me, neither."

"But you came close?"

"You mean with Travis? We discussed marriage a couple of times, but honestly, both of us realized the strong commitment just wasn't there. And maybe the love. Do you ... have anyone, Neal?" She held her breath until he answered.

"No."

"Only the blonde in the photo?"

He nodded. "No one since her. No one important."

They rode quietly until he pulled to a stop beside the clinic. Gwyn felt a pang of disappointment that the evening was almost over. It had been such fun to escape with Neal. For a while she could forget that they worked together, that they had exchanged heated words and clashed over ideas. Tonight had been a blending, a glorious meshing of their spirits. It had been wonderful.

Slowly they climbed the porch steps and entered the living quarters. With the door closed and locked, they stood for a moment in the dark. She was very conscious of his warm presence so close to her, of his eyes penetrating the darkness, seeking hers.

He moved a step toward her, his gaze locked on her face. Shrugging out of his jacket, he reached for hers. Never letting his gaze falter, he dropped the coats on a chair and moved closer to her. She could hear his breath, feel his body heat. His hands gently touched her arms, then scooted up to rest on her shoulders. His power swirled around them, engulfing her in his strong attraction, pulling them closer.

"Gwyn ..." He uttered her name in a whisper.

"Yes ..." She responded the only way she could. *Yes! Oh, yes, please kiss me!*

He drew her to him. She felt his masculine power, the strength of his hands on her shoulders, the press of his pelvis hard against hers. She was overwhelmed by the aphrodisiac of his mossy fragrance and, with a purely unconscious effort, reached out to him. She heard, or rather felt, his quick intake of air as her hands rested on his ribs. Touching him, she felt his heat. The erotic thoughts that his heat was meant for her sent Gwyn's senses soaring, and she swayed toward him.

Her lips trembled, begged wordlessly, for his steadying kiss. The pause the moment before their lips merged seemed endless. She could feel his sweet breath mingling with hers, almost feel soft lips on hers. And she thought she'd die if he didn't complete the act.

Harboring no further hesitation, his mouth forged with amazing fervor with hers, molding, moving hungrily. But it was no less hungry than hers as she met his kiss with a strength of her own.

He sought her with more passion than she'd ever known. And she responded with more willingness than she'd ever believed possible. She melted against him, softened beneath his heat, wanted more. He didn't lift his head until they were both breathless and clinging to each other.

He sighed raggedly. "Gwyn, I . . ."

She pressed two fingers to his lips. "Please don't regret this. It just happened, that's all."

"I shouldn't let something like this happen."

"Frankly, Doctor, I don't think you had any control over this."

"Does that give you pleasure? A feeling of power over me?"

"Yes. I wanted that kiss, too." She stroked his cheek with her fingertips. "You read my mind."

"I've wanted to taste your lips since that first night you arrived."

"How do I taste?"

"Like wine. Sweet and—oh, Gwyn." He straightened.

"You liked it as much as I did. Why deny it, Neal?"

"Because I . . . I haven't done that in so long."

"Kissed a woman?"

"Wanted a woman the way I want you. Not in so long." He shuddered and pushed on her shoulders, putting a small space between them as if he didn't trust himself anymore.

"It's no sin, Neal."

"We're so different, Gwyn. It would never work."

She closed his lips with her fingers again. "What wouldn't work? The kiss? Well, I thought it worked quite well. I'm sufficiently breathless. And you?"

"More than breathless," he mumbled.

"Good. I'll admit to wanting that kiss . . . *your kiss*, Neal." She stepped back, and their embrace was completely broken. "I don't see anything wrong with that."

He stared at her. He'd never met anyone like her, never experienced such an overwhelming urge for passion. Never thought he'd feel this way for a woman again. He chalked it up to lust.

She smiled in the darkness. "Thanks for a perfectly lovely evening. I enjoyed every moment. Even—especially—the kiss."

He remained perfectly still when she started to go. Then she reconsidered and slowly turned around. She stood before him on tiptoe, hands braced on his upper arms, and kissed him squarely on the mouth again. Then she backed away one step and gave him a self-satisfied smile. "Just because I wanted to, that's why."

And before she succumbed to her own wildly raging desires, Gwyn fled to her room.

5

THAT KISS! Nothing else mattered to Neal at this moment except that kiss. Not the clinic, not the people in his life or hers, not his memories, just the way he felt when they touched. On fire. She felt it, too. He knew by her response, by the way she pressed against him and opened her arms and quivered when their lips met. Oh, he could die for another kiss like that—or at least lose sleep over it.

He stared out the window into the moonless, black night. The dusty smell of new gravel was still in the air, but Gwyn's exotic fragrance lingered in his senses. She was dangerously sexy! Dangerous for both of them! She was enough to ruin a man like him. To make him want to run away with her, away from his commitments, from his dedication, from his past.

He chuckled sarcastically. She probably wouldn't go because it wasn't on her schedule. How do you log in running away? Gwyn was probably too sensible to do something wildly spontaneous.

She was so goal oriented, accomplishing worthwhile objectives like improving the parking lot with a load of gravel, which would mean no more mud in the winter. He was convinced Gwyn was behind it. Even if the others had come up with the plan, she was responsible. She was behind all the changes around here. Even his own.

Neal flung himself into bed and willed himself to sleep. But all he could think of was burying his hands deep into her dark hair, touching her smooth face, her neck, her breasts, and another kiss . . . and another. . . .

GWYN STARED at the ceiling in the dark. Now this was a real time waster, one of the worst. Born of frustration, her reasons for not sleeping centered on one man. And not the right man! This one was there quite by accident and his powerful influence wouldn't leave her so easily.

Logically she knew she should get up and do something. She could read or otherwise make use of the time. But she was in a daze, remembering, *reliving* that kiss!

No one had ever kissed her like that. Or left her feeling so torn and disrupted. So crazy and wild. Oh, how she wanted to march over to Neal's bedroom, fling open the door and demand, "Kiss me like that again!"

She knew, though, that they wouldn't stop at another kiss. And the way she felt right now, she didn't care. Not about her job or obligations back in Chicago, not about Neal's job or his past—nothing but them, melding in an erotic frenzy. Oh, dear, this was dangerous! And downright crazy!

She had to stop thinking—to stop dreaming about Dr. Neal Perry—had to get some sleep. Gwyn turned onto her side and tried to forget the gentle brush of his beard on her face, the sensuous mating of his lips with hers. But invading her subconscious was a growing surge of overwhelming desire for this special man. In frustration she squeezed her knees together. But nothing quenched the wildfire burning deep within her. Only another kiss would . . . and another. . . .

THE NEXT MORNING they slept too late to jog. Gwyn heard familiar noises and, pulling on her robe, shuffled into the kitchen. She mumbled a greeting without looking directly at Neal. How could she meet those devastating blue eyes of his this morning?

Neal fixed the coffee, acutely aware of the uncomfortable silence between them. What should he say? *Thoughts of that kiss kept me awake half the night!*

Gwyn mixed some frozen orange juice and poured it into two small glasses. She'd never felt so awkward— and speechless—in her life. She wondered, *why did you have to kiss me like that?*

The phone rang and both of them jumped.

Neal answered it. A male voice asked for Gwyn. He knew it wasn't her boss. "For you."

She looked at Neal, her deep brown eyes meeting his steady gaze for the first time that morning. And she felt again the warm rush his kiss had given her. She took a shaky breath and mustered a smile. It seemed to take forever for her to cross the room and reach for the phone. "Hello?"

"Hi, Gwyn! How's it going in the backwoods?"

"Oh, fine, Trav. Everything's smooth." She felt anything but smooth right now.

"Are you getting their systems organized?"

"Mmm-hmm, trying."

"I'm calling from Milwaukee. Having a great week! Tell you all about it when we both get back to Chicago. I'm due now at a power breakfast...."

Travis droned on and Gwyn listened, saying the obligatory things, answering the way she should, trying not to think of the day she would be finished here and heading home.

She hung up and looked across the room at Neal. He made no attempt to hide the fact that he'd listened to her side of the conversation. She turned her face away, unable to think of any sensible explanation. It was all too confusing right now.

She hadn't expected to like it here or to care if she could make any improvements at Harmony Creek. But most of all, she hadn't expected to be so darned attracted to the handsome doctor. She hadn't expected his kiss to upset her so much that it had kept her awake half the night. She hadn't expected to want more of Neal.

Neal poured two cups of coffee and placed one on the table, motioning silently at her.

She smiled gratefully and moved toward it, feeling as if she were striding in slow motion through Jell-O. When she reached the table, she sat down and hunched over the cup of steaming coffee. Wrapping her hands around it, she stared bleakly into the black brew. "That was Travis," she said finally, unnecessarily.

"I gathered." Neal stood with his back to her, busy slicing bananas over two bowls of cereal.

"I can't think of going back."

"Then don't."

"That call reminded me where I belong." She sighed and slapped her thigh. "Ah, what's one little kiss?"

He glanced over and picked up on her denial. "It was just a brief moment in time. A weak one at that."

"That's what I thought." She nodded in agreement and sipped her coffee. Suddenly she felt betrayed by his flip remark.

He turned around to face her. "That's a lie."

She looked up, her gaze meeting his. Thank God! She nodded ever so slightly. "I'm afraid so."

"Look, I didn't intend to kiss you." *Didn't mean to kiss you like that!*

"I know. Me, neither. It just happened." *And I just happened to respond!*

"It won't happen again. I swear, Gwyn."

"Don't say that. I mean—" She thought she'd die if she could never again feel his lips on hers. "Please, Neal. I'm not blaming you. It was me, too."

"I'm glad you know."

"I know how I felt last night. How I feel now."

"And how's that?"

She took a deep breath and smiled faintly. "Confused."

"I know what you mean." He set a bowl of cereal before her and ambled to the front window, gazing unseeingly out at the freshly graveled parking lot while he ate. After a time he asked, "What's really between you and Travis?"

Gwyn gazed at Neal's broad-shouldered back, remembering the taut muscles, wanting to feel them beneath her exploring hands. With no control over her emotions, she was reliving the kiss, wanting more. "Nothing. I told you, we're just friends."

"Then why does he keep calling?"

"He's the team leader in my department. It's his job to keep in touch with me."

"Okay." He turned around and smiled at her. His blue eyes sparked. "I can deal with that."

She angled her head. "Do I detect a bit of jealousy, Doctor?"

He shrugged. "Naw. What's to be jealous of? One little kiss? It was nothing."

Nothing? It had kept her awake for hours, and he called it "nothing"! Gwyn dug into her cereal. She had to decide what to do about these new feelings. Should she deny them and chalk them up to a mere lusty attraction to this extremely appealing man? Could she proceed to stay on track and do her job, working with Neal and feeling nothing? Or would he let the repercussions of one kiss mess up her life plan— "Who's out there?" Neal had heard something and peered out the window. "A couple of men look like they're measuring the steps."

"Oh. That's probably Henry Waddell."

He looked at her curiously, then turned back to the window. "Yes, I believe it is old Henry and his son-in-law, Aaron. What—" He turned around to Gwyn, folding his arms and drumming his fingers, waiting for an answer. Undoubtedly she knew what those two were doing at the clinic at this hour of the morning. Her weak smile and guilty expression said she did. "Okay, Gwyn. Shoot. What's going on this time?"

She cleared her throat and began encouragingly. "They're going to build a ramp on one side of the steps. Isn't it wonderful? Look, Neal, I know what you're thinking, but it was their idea to do something positive for the clinic, something really needed. As well as to cut into their family bill. So, when I learned they were out-of-work carpenters, I made a couple of suggestions."

"Did it have something to do with the Waddells not wanting to be outdone by the Nelsons?"

"A little competition never hurts." She shrugged. "And you must admit, you need better access to the clinic. You definitely should have facilities for the handicapped."

"Yes, I'll admit we need a lot of things." Neal walked toward her, a slow grin spreading over his dark face.

"But mostly I think we've needed a powerhouse like Gwyn Frederick for a long time. I have, anyway."

"You aren't mad?"

"Why should I be?"

She shrugged. "It's another surprise."

"You're full of them, it seems. In more ways than one."

She blushed. "Neal, last night wasn't in the plan. Surely you know that."

He studied her for a moment. "Any other surprises today?"

"Just the visit from Representative Sanders. But you know about that. Now you can't blame me for this political maneuver. I had absolutely nothing to do with it, even though I'm with the SHARE program and that's what he wants to talk about. He would have done this no matter who had come."

"I'm not blaming you for any of this, Gwyn. I'm learning to take the surprises as they come and not place blame or credit." He grinned. "Funny thing, though. When you aren't here, everything is dull and ordinary."

"Except for the unplanned crises," she reminded him.

"Right." He chuckled. "Any idea what time our venerable representative will honor us with his presence?"

"I expect early, so that whatever he says or does can make the evening news."

Neal finished his coffee and set his cup down on the counter. He placed the two bowls of cereal on the table. "We'd better get dressed. Looks like a long, busy day."

She grinned, and in that moment Gwyn knew she didn't regret being here with Neal, the kiss or even one sleepless moment because of it.

WHEN THE STATE REPRESENTATIVE arrived with his entourage, Neal was busy setting a little girl's arm. Up to his armpits in plaster, he called on Gwyn. "Who are all those people trailing around after him?"

"The media," she said with an encouraging smile.

"A TV camera?"

"Of course. That's the most important news. Reaches the most viewers."

Neal shook his head and continued his messy job. "I can't see much use in any of this."

"Oh, but there is, Neal. It could be very beneficial."

"To us? Or the newscast?"

"To us." She gave him a sly look. "Just let me handle it."

"Be my guest." Neal looked relieved as she left the room and greeted the troupe in her confident, businesslike manner.

Gwyn extended her hand. "Welcome to Harmony Creek Clinic, Representative Sanders. I'm Gwyn Frederick, here on assignment through the SHARE program."

"Nice to meet you, Ms Frederick." He pumped her hand, then introduced her to the two reporters at his elbows and to his administrative assistant, who hovered one step away. "I want to talk with you," he said. "We'd like to know all about this SHARE program from one who is actually participating. Your feelings, opinions, observations, that sort of thing. On camera, of course. While they're setting up, I'll just . . ." He wandered around the waiting room, shaking hands with the waiting patients.

Ever the politician, Gwyn thought as she watched him work the small bunch. Never miss an opportunity to shake hands. *You want my opinions, Representative? You've got them, sir! Maybe more than you bargained for!*

She watched as more folks gathered curiously outside the clinic, thanks to a speedy grapevine and quick recognition of the news van with its bold call letters written on all sides. Well, she'd bide her time. Gwyn had her own plan for the interview. It was an opportunity she wouldn't miss. *He may be ever the politician*, she mused, *but I'm ever the opportunist. This system can work both ways.*

When smiling Representative Sanders returned to her, she said, "I'll be glad to talk with you on camera. I have some specific observations and needs to discuss."

"Excellent. Just save them for now." He turned to the reporters, who were always on his heels. "Could we get a sweeping shot of the waiting room? And the doctor at work?" He looked questioningly at Gwyn.

She nodded. "That probably could be arranged."

"And those fellows outside. What are they building?"

"A ramp for the disabled." Gwyn spoke pointedly. "It's something the government should have provided for a public building such as this clinic. But somehow Harmony Creek has slipped between the cracks of bureaucracy. Since no one else seems to care, these members of the community are doing the job."

"Why, uh, you're absolutely right, young lady," the representative said in a blustering fashion, motioning impatiently to the cameraman. "Get a shot of those men at work, please."

"Then their work is volunteered?" one of the reporters asked Gwyn, writing as he spoke.

"I think 'donated' is a better word," Gwyn answered. "They wanted to contribute something worthwhile to the clinic, to repay in some way the valuable services provided here." She smiled with self-satisfaction as the reporters scribbled down her every word.

The curious visitors seemed to be everywhere at once, conducting interviews, taking still shots and shooting film, and generally getting in the way of the medical services. They even taped Neal putting the finishing touches on the little girl's cast and obtained a brief statement from him on the needs of the clinic. Then they quickly moved to Gwyn.

"Tell us exactly how the SHARE program works, Ms Frederick," Representative Sanders began after introducing her to the TV audience.

"It's a way for a private sector to contribute much-needed services, most of them business oriented, to government agencies. The particular company contracts for several weeks' work with specifically chosen agencies. In theory, it's supposed to be a sharing of information, innovative ideas and services. Sometimes, though, as in this case, the company is merely assigned with no consideration to the specific needs of the government agency." Gwyn knew that would get the politician's attention. She noted the newspaper reporter was recording, as well as taking copious notes.

"No consideration, eh? How so? What does your company do?"

"I'm from Mark Time Inc. of Chicago. We're a time management firm. We do time-and-motion studies of businesses and show them how they can cut wasted effort and improve productivity." She spoke with enthusiasm. "Harmony Creek Clinic has only one doctor, and frankly, my organizational skills can do only so much. The doctor is pretty overworked. He requested nursing assistance and needs help desperately. Instead of filling his specific requests, they sent help he didn't need."

"Well." Representative Sanders gaped at her. Obviously the answer she'd given wasn't the one he'd expected. Or wanted. He was forced to respond. "We'll have to look into this."

Gwyn smiled tolerantly. *This* was the reaction she wanted. "I think you should, Representative Sanders, if you really want to help these people."

"Of course I do," he sputtered. "They're my main concern. Uh, that's why we're working so hard to get approval to replace that bridge before next winter."

"I don't know about a bridge, but I do know that the main road from Ducktown needs repair."

The representative adjusted his tie. "You're right about that, too. That road is in terrible disrepair. We'll look into the matter."

"Perhaps if you talked to the road commissioner?"

"Of course. We will, first chance. You're very observant, Ms Frederick. Sometimes it takes an outsider like you to make such observations."

"It doesn't take much to see that the doctor needs help, though."

"Thank you, Ms Frederick." The representative smiled into the camera, effectively ending the taped interview.

Gwyn moved away from the spotlight, only then realizing the full impact of what she'd said. She'd been tough, maybe too tough. What if, by her pointedness, she'd made the situation worse? She'd been rather assertive, especially for a woman in the South. Biting her lower lip, she glanced up to see Neal watching her. He'd been leaning against the doorjamb of one of the examining rooms, listening to her interview.

She searched his face for an expression of disapproval. To her great relief, his usually grim face was smiling. Her heart leaped, and she responded with a tight grin.

Neal made an okay sign with his thumb and forefinger and disappeared inside the room. In that glorious moment Gwyn knew she'd done all right, that Neal was satisfied. To her, his approval was all that mattered.

Eventually the media crews began to pack to leave. The representative went around smiling and shaking hands with the folks who'd gathered. Gwyn walked him out to the car, trying to soften her attack by chatting about the local delights of food and weather as compared to those in Chicago. But before he got into the car, she grew serious and steered the conversation back on track.

"I hope you'll do something about hiring a nurse for the clinic. They also need an office manager, considering all the paperwork," she said.

"We'll do everything we can."

"There are problems with filling this position that you should be aware of, Representative Sanders. This isn't a regular job. And it will take an exceptional person to fill it. Someone who is willing to accept the remoteness of the area as well as the low salary."

"I'll keep that in mind."

"Please listen. I have a suggestion."

He looked at her with raised eyebrows. He obviously wanted to rid himself of her as quickly as possible.

But Gwyn wouldn't be pushed aside. "I aim for solutions, sir. And this just might work."

He placated her with a smile and a rather forced expression of attention.

"Check with the area nursing schools. See if they have graduates who prefer to live and work in a rural setting, rather than a city hospital. Perhaps there's someone who needs or wants a job like this."

"I'll have my assistant look into it."

"I'll check with your office next week to see if you've made any progress." Her expression said he'd hear from her until he did something about the problem. And from the way she'd conducted herself today, he knew she obviously wouldn't be shy about speaking to the media about this issue.

Representative Sanders seemed to become a bit more receptive. "You're persistent, Ms Frederick. But you have good ideas. I like that."

"Thank you, sir. I'll be in touch." Gwyn smiled warmly and waved as his car drove away, wondering if Harmony Creek would ever see results from her pleas. But she just couldn't give up.

Now she could see why Neal was less than receptive to the news media and not particularly impressed with someone of her credentials. She was a pawn, someone to be used in the system. And still the politicians came around to placate the public, bringing the news media hungry for a story. All they were interested in was making an impact on the evening news. They gathered their information, then drove away before sundown, leaving the problems intact. It just wasn't fair.

Well, she'd stay longer than sundown and try to make an impact before she left. That would be her contribution to Harmony Creek Clinic, even if it wasn't terribly organized when she left. Kicking at the new gravel, she turned around and headed back to the clinic.

Henry Waddell, one of the men building the ramp, approached her. "We're almost finished here. Tomorrow we'll be back to install a railing on each side. Would you tell the doctor, Ms Frederick?"

Gwyn nodded and walked over to the new construction. "This is an excellent job, gentlemen," she said with an approving smile.

"We hope Dr. Perry likes it," Henry said as he helped his son-in-law put away their tools.

"I'm sure he will," she said, walking onto the ramp. "There are so many patients who will benefit from your work. It's going to fill a great need for the clinic."

"Good. We'd do anything we could to help Dr. Perry, because he does such a great job for us." Henry paused. "Did you know he saved my granny's life the very day he arrived here?"

"No, Henry, I didn't know that."

"Yep," he said with a twist to his lips. "She had a heart attack in the middle of the night, and the doc had her airlifted to intensive care in Chattanooga. She'll be eighty-eight next month because of him. Fine man, he is."

"I agree." A strange feeling of warmth spread over Gwyn. This man whose kiss had kept her awake half the night was, indeed, a special person. "I'd like to meet your grandmother someday. Thank you for your work." She shook hands with both Henry and Aaron.

"Don't forget to watch the news tonight. I'm sure it'll make your grandmother proud. I'll bet you two are the stars of the show!" She felt there was a good chance her entire conversation with Representative Sanders would be cut because it had been controversial. She didn't really care, as long as he fulfilled her requests.

The men grinned at each other and swelled with pride. Gwyn knew that news of the success of this job would spread. And she hoped others would want to do something to outshine the ramp and the gravel. But she was realistic enough to know that the man with the real power to get something done was Representative Sanders. She just hoped she'd put enough pressure and instilled enough community interest to get action.

That evening she and Neal went to the McPhersons' for dinner. While they waited for the TV news, Gwyn admitted she wasn't a nurse. She detected a gleam in Mae's eyes and knew the older lady has visions of Gwyn keeping Neal from being so lonely.

"I don't care. You're almost like a nurse," Mae said sweetly. "You do such a good job of everything."

"Here, here," Neal agreed with a teasing grin for Gwyn.

"Quiet!" Jed pointed at the TV. "This is it!"

They laughed when the camera showed the doctor working on the little girl's cast, just before he turned his back on the camera and tripped over some lighting cords. They were delighted with shots of the Waddells building the handicap ramp and views of the newly graveled parking lot and clinic waiting room that included several familiar faces. But when Gwyn appeared on screen, they watched in quiet awe. She fairly glowed on camera.

"You're a natural, Gwyn," Mae said. "You must have experience at that sort of thing back in Chicago."

"No, this was the first time I've ever been on TV," Gwyn said. "I tried to ignore the camera and lights because I had something to say. And I said it."

"You certainly did," Neal said with a chuckle.

"I'm amazed more of my interview wasn't cut," she admitted. "The real test will be if there are any results."

"You might be surprised," Mae said, dishing up her famous stew. "Paul Sanders grew up in Ducktown, so his roots are close. He's always worked hard for the people around here. Look how he's fighting to get the bridge built."

"Fighting is right," Jed said, pouring everyone a glass of rich blackberry wine. "The whole state's against it."

"What's this about? What bridge?" Gwyn placed the bowls of steaming stew on the table.

"They're calling it the 'bridge to nowhere,'" Jed added with a chuckle.

"But we all know it goes somewhere!" Mae said. "Don't we, Neal?"

"You bet," Neal agreed. "I think Sanders'll get it done. He seems determined enough to do it."

"Where does it go?" Gwyn insisted.

"To the mountain," Mae said, handing Gwyn the napkins. "It was washed out in the flood of '86. Paul Sanders is fighting for the rights to federal funds given to help the flood victims to rebuild their bridge."

"There's a great hue and cry against it, though," Neal said.

"Why?" Gwyn asked.

"There are claims that there aren't enough people living on Buck Mountain to benefit from such an extravagant use of tax money."

"How many live there?"

"About a hundred."

"That isn't very many for a multimillion dollar bridge."

"But I contend that numbers aren't important. People are." Neal's strong conviction was reflected in his expression. "To me, human need surpasses cost effectiveness."

Jed, who had said little all evening, added a bit of history. "The old-time settlers of Buck Mountain built the first bridge almost a hundred years ago. In the thirties the C.C.C. boys rebuilt it with logs from that very mountain. Now it needs to be replaced again. Seems to me the government should take care of it, seeing as how it was destroyed by an act of nature. But the city folks want to use the money, probably to build more of them condos."

"I see," Gwyn said thoughtfully. "But you understand how the benefits of the majority must be considered. As a businessperson I can see their point."

"Not me." Neal stood his ground stubbornly. "As a humanitarian I can see only that real people need that bridge. Anyway, the money's there for that purpose, waiting for approval. Unfortunately the outcry against the bridge has delayed action."

"Could we eat now, folks?" Mae suggested, taking Gwyn's hand and leading her to the table. "Before we get into an argument over this?"

They let the subject drop. But Gwyn wondered why Neal was so blind about something that was so clearly a political debacle. Every businessperson and politician knew that sometimes emotion had to be abandoned in order to achieve greater goals. Maybe if they forgot about the bridge, they'd eventually gain more for Harmony Creek.

After finishing huge quantities of Mae's terrific beef stew and corn bread, they played gin rummy until nearly midnight. But when they left, Neal didn't drive directly home. He took the narrow, winding ridge road.

"Where are we going?"

"I want to show you something." He pulled the Jeep to a stop alongside several cars with windows so steamed they couldn't see the occupants.

"You wanted to show me Lover's Lane, Neal?"

"It was a lookout point before it was Lover's Lane. It's called Eagle Ridge because you get an eagle's view from here."

She settled back in her seat and let her gaze sweep the heavens, where clouds bunched and moved across the sliver of a moon. Occasionally they completely blocked sight of it. "Lovely," she said in a quiet voice.

He shifted forward, motioning her to do the same, and pointed out various familiar spots. "Murphy lies on the other side of that mountain. Ducktown's over there. Directly below are the clinic and home sweet home. Other side of the woods, the actual Harmony Creek, or 'crick,' as the locals say. And across it, Buck Mountain. And there—" he leaned closer to her "—is where the 'bridge to nowhere' goes."

Gwyn looked down to the rushing, dark waters where aeons ago the stream carved its niche between the mountain and the ridge. Today it continued its course, rushing off to join the Ocoee River. "It's beautiful, isn't it?"

"As innocent and beautiful as it looks now, it floods often, causing tremendous hardships for those who live on the other side."

"How do they get across when it floods?"

"They don't."

He started the Jeep, and they drove back in silence. It was raining by the time they reached the clinic. They'd left a lamp on, and the yellow glow was warm and welcoming as they dashed inside.

"Can I get you anything?" Neal offered.

"No, thanks. After what I ate tonight, I may never be hungry again."

"Before you go, I'd like to correct something you said in that interview today."

"What's that?" She took off her coat, heart suddenly pounding. He disapproved of something. She *knew* she'd been too aggressive.

He took his coat off and hung it on the coat rack beside hers. "You said you were sent to provide help I don't need." He shook his head. "Wrong, Gwyn. I think I need you more than anything."

She laughed. "What for? To disrupt your life and fill it with schedules and complications and surprises?"

He grinned. "All that only keeps me on my toes. Just look at what you've gotten accomplished in less than a week."

She tried to make light of her efforts. "After I got over not wanting to be here, I figured I should leave this place better than I found it."

"You definitely are." He moved closer and reached up to tug softly on one of her twisted curls. "We're all much better for your having been here. I'm already dreading your leaving."

"You'll have your privacy back."

"It'll be dull and lonely."

"But you liked it alone a week ago."

"That was before..." He halted and let one finger trail down her silky, soft cheek. "Before this." His lips caressed hers lightly; his beard gently brushed her chin. He hovered, looking at her with a depth of passion he couldn't hide. "Ah, Gwyn, you're turning me inside out."

"Neal—" Uncharacteristically she was plagued with indecision. She couldn't think of a good reason not to fall into his arms. Finally she mumbled, "If it weren't so impossible for us . . ."

He straightened and looked into her eyes. "You're right. We're just temporary, aren't we?"

"I'm afraid so." Gwyn nodded and lowered her eyelids. He was so close she could feel his energy, smell his woodsy fragrance. Even though she knew it was a mistake, she wanted him to kiss her again.

Neal looked at those thick, black lashes feathering Gwyn's cheeks, hiding her luscious brown eyes. He wanted to taste her again, wanted to touch her. But all he could do was inhale her marvelously exotic fragrance, the one he'd remembered all night. It took all his willpower to keep from sweeping her up in his arms and carrying her into his bedroom. But she'd said it herself. Impossible!

Feeling a mounting frustration, Neal reached for the lamp. Gwyn shifted at the same time to move away from him. In the confusion she tripped over his foot. He reached for her, steadying her against him. And she gratefully clutched him. Their eyes met and locked. Immediate, undeniable desire flared between them.

"You're the time expert," he said. "Aren't you supposed to arrange time for pleasure?"

"Yes."

"Then let's not spoil a perfectly nice evening by halting the pleasure."

"Maybe you're right," she agreed with a soft laugh.

It was the gentle nudge he needed. With a longing beyond belief he swept her into his arms. His lips closed over hers. There was an urgency in the kiss, a seeking, even a demanding. She murmured softly as he forced his tongue inside the honeyed depths, past her teeth to taste her sweetness.

When he raised his head, his whisper was low and hoarse. "Gwyn, I want more. Want you."

"Me, too, Neal. I can't help it."

"That's all I want to hear." He kissed her again, long and deep and leaving them both breathless. "Stay, Gwyn. Stay with me."

"Yes." Her voice was a whisper of yearning.

Without a word he lifted her in his arms and carried her to his bed. Almost as soon as she hit the pillow, he began discarding their clothes. Their sweaters were piled on the floor, their boots tossed aside. As if he couldn't wait to see all of her, he unclasped her bra. Cupping her breasts with gentle hands, he bathed each with kisses.

She arched and lay back on the bed as he took each firm nipple into his mouth, sucking gently until the tips were hard and aching. His hands fumbled with the waistband on her slacks—and a pounding could be heard. At first Gwyn thought it was her own heart. She throbbed all over with desire.

Neal halted and lifted his head. "Who's that?"

She felt coolness as he moved away from her. "What is it?"

"Someone at the door. I'll see."

She could hear an exchange of anxious voices, then Neal returned to the room. She sat up curiously, pulling a blanket to her bare breasts. "Something wrong, Neal?"

"I'm needed on the mountain." He heaved himself down on the edge of the bed and began tugging on his boots again. "They're about a week early."

In the semidarkness, she could see the marvelous muscled expanse of his bare back and longed to touch it again. To feel his chest crushing her breasts. "What is it?"

"Would you like to see what a country doc really does for a living?"

"Well, yes . . ."

"Then get dressed! Quick!"

6

GWYN FUMBLED with her bra. The urgency in his voice was contagious, and she dressed with that same compelling fervor. "What is it, Neal?"

"I should have expected it. A little ahead of schedule, but normal. I hope." He retrieved his shirt from the floor and turned to face her as he buttoned it. He was smiling. "Debra Hancock's in labor."

"Oh, someone's having a baby." Gwyn couldn't mask her disappointment. "Is this her first?"

"No, it's her fifth pregnancy. And she's not having *a* baby. It's twins." He tucked in his shirt and adjusted his belt.

Gwyn's gaze followed his hands as they reached inside his waistband. "Shouldn't they take her to the hospital?"

"I tried to persuade her, but she refused. She had all the others at home and wants these to be born there, too. Anyway, the hospital's in Murphy. It would be a difficult trip, plus a great inconvenience to her family. Also, there's the expense." He shook his head. "So I'll do the best I can. I'm concerned about her age, though."

"How old is she?"

"Forty-one." He picked their sweaters off the floor and tossed hers on the bed. "Better dress warmly. It's always colder on Buck Mountain. I have to get some medicine and equipment. Hurry up if you're coming with me."

"Would you like me to come?"

"Yes! I'll need all the help I can get!"

"Then I'm coming."

He paused at the door. "Better bring an extra blanket. We might need it."

Gwyn's heart pounded as she pulled her sweater over her head. She could hear the rain pelting the roof and dreaded going out into the cold, wet night. But she couldn't let him go alone. He'd said he needed her.

She sat on the edge of Neal's bed, staring into the darkness. What had happened to them tonight? Right now it seemed as if the passion had never happened. He was alert and concentrating on other things, other people, while she was dazed and still wishing his arms were around her.

What in the world was she thinking to allow herself to be carried off to Neal's bed like some character in a movie? Was she absolutely nuts? She had to go back to Chicago soon, and yet she had been willing to go to bed with Neal!

But a tiny voice deep inside reminded her that no one had ever made her feel the way Neal did.

Gwyn scrambled around the floor, searching for her boots. When she emerged from Neal's bedroom, dressed and carrying the extra blanket, she encountered a teenager helping Neal load supplies.

"Billy Joe, Debra's eldest son, came after me. Billy Joe, this is Gwyn Frederick, my, uh..." Neal paused for only a moment. "My assistant." He headed out to the Jeep with a box, leaving them alone to mumble greetings.

For a moment Gwyn was embarrassed to be seen coming from Neal's bedroom. She wanted to say, "It's not what you think. We didn't do anything!" But she

knew that their passion would have carried them away
if they hadn't been interrupted by this emergency. Then
it occurred to her that Billy Joe wouldn't know which
door led to Neal's bedroom. Plus he probably didn't
even care what she was doing. He was obviously too
worried about his mother to be concerned with anyone else. Gwyn's guilty conscience was working over-
time.

Suddenly she felt compassion for the youth, and her
feelings went beyond her own, compelling her to reassure him. That seemed to be part of an assistant's role.
"It's going to be all right, Billy Joe. The doctor knows
just what to do."

"Yes, ma'am. Could we hurry?"

"Sure." She donned her coat and handed Neal his.
Soon they were driving through the rain behind the
Hancocks' old pickup truck. When they came to a
rushing body of water that poured over the road, Billy
Joe merely splashed headlong into it.

Gwyn grabbed Neal's arm. "Wait! We aren't going
in there, are we?"

Neal downshifted. "It's the only way. Don't worry,
the water level's still low. This is the invisible bridge to
nowhere." He drove right into the creek. "It would be
nice to have a bridge, don't you think?"

Gwyn recoiled in her seat, instinctively drawing her
feet up as if they might get wet on the floorboard. She
peered through her window at the swirling waters beneath them. "Ohh, I don't like this!"

"The folks who live on Buck Mountain make this trip
daily. And they don't like it, either."

She didn't release her viselike grip on his arm—and
start breathing again—until they were safely on the

other side. "Thank goodness!" She breathed a sigh of relief and tried to settle down again.

"I just hope the water doesn't rise too high for us to get back across."

Gwyn glared at Neal in the darkness. They weren't safe yet! "What'll we do if we can't cross it?"

Neal didn't answer. He concentrated on the dirt road, which was rapidly turning to slick mud. She didn't press for a response, not wanting to divert his attention from his task. He was somber and quiet, obviously preoccupied. Apparently he'd forgotten their brief moment of passion. Although she tried, Gwyn couldn't get those feelings out of her mind. Or her heart.

After thirty minutes of winding up the narrow roadway carved into the side of the mountain, they arrived at a small house nestled in a circle of trees. One side of the house was dark and peaceful, but the other side was well lit and ready for activity. The children were probably sleeping, while the adults prepared for the birth of more children. A lanky, weathered man swept the door open and met Neal on the porch, urging him to hurry.

By the time Gwyn dashed through the rain and stepped into the house, Neal had disappeared. Apparently he was with the patient. She faced the tall man, who looked haggard and worried, much like the teenager who came after them. "Mr. Hancock? I'm Gwyn Frederick, the, uh, doctor's assistant." She quickly decided that while not exactly accurate, calling herself an assistant was the simplest explanation.

"I'm W.T. My wife's have a baby. No, two of 'em! Hope everything's all right in there." He paced the room and motioned to the sofa. "Have a seat, ma'am."

"No, thank you. I'm not here to visit. I'm here to help, W.T.," she said gently. "Uh, what do you need me to do?"

He stared at her distractedly. "I don't . . ."

"Why don't I make some coffee?" Gwyn could see she would have to take charge. "And do you have a big pot for boiling water?"

"Uh, sure." He motioned vaguely toward the kitchen. "In there."

She gave the expectant father a reassuring smile. "If it'll help any, I want you to know that Dr. Perry is very competent. And he really cares about your wife and the babies. In fact, he cares about all of you." Neal had proved that to her in many ways all week. But especially tonight.

W.T. blinked nervously, then his serious expression softened a bit. "Thanks, ma'am. That does help. I've been mighty worried about Debra all along. But the folks around here say Dr. Perry's the best doctor they've seen."

Gwyn reached out and spontaneously gave his rough hand a little squeeze. "I wouldn't doubt that a bit. Now, where's the kitchen?"

"Billy Joe, show this lady where things are."

For the next twenty minutes Gwyn and young Billy Joe devoted themselves to the kitchen. They made coffee, started water boiling, cleaned up a sinkful of dirty dishes and chatted about school and Billy Joe's hobby of wood carving. It was a brief diversion in what promised to be a long, tension-filled night. When they heard Neal's voice, Billy Joe edged to the doorway to listen.

Gwyn gave his shoulder a gentle push. "Go on in. The doctor knows you're concerned about your mom." She followed the boy into the living room.

"It's going to be a little while yet." Neal's expression and attitude were positive and reassuring. "W.T., you and Billy Joe can go in and see Debra. It'll make her feel better to know you're here. Reassure her everything's going fine, just as expected. She's doing great."

"I can't thank you enough for coming out on a night like this, Doc," W.T. said. "I don't know what we'd have done if you hadn't been home."

Neal clapped him on the back and chuckled. "You'd get Mae McPherson or one of the other women in the community and y'all would deliver some babies. Now, while you're in there, if she has a contraction, a labor pain, don't panic. Let her squeeze your hand, and tell her in a calm voice to breathe the way I told her. Stay calm. That's the key." He glanced over at Gwyn. "Do I smell coffee?"

She nodded.

The men started toward Debra's room, and Neal followed Gwyn into the kitchen. She handed him a steaming cup.

"Ah, this is great." He took a deep breath and a sip of the black brew.

"How is she? Really?"

"Holding up well, under the circumstances. The labor's been going on so long now she's quite tired. I gave her something to help her rest between contractions. But I want her awake for the births. Fortunately we've got a little time before the action. It'll give us a chance to get organized. You'll like this part." He grinned teasingly at her, then noticed the steaming pot of water on

the stove. "Are you sure you've never done this before?"

She responded with a smile. "I saw this in a movie
once. It kept Billy Joe and me busy. I think that's the
main function for boiling water, isn't it? He's very worried, you know. Refused to go to bed."

"Well, he's sixteen and getting a taste of real life.
That's why I sent them both in to see her. It may be several hours before she's fully dilated. Meanwhile we have
our work cut out for us. I'm going to need all the help
I can get on this, Gwyn. Can I count on you?"

"Of course, Neal." She smiled proudly at him. "That
is, I'll do what I can to help, which I'm afraid won't be
much. But I'll keep the coffee flowing and—"

"Gwyn, I need more than that," he interrupted sol-
emnly. "Have you ever seen a birth?"

"I watched my cat have kittens when I was thirteen."
She chuckled nervously. "Why? You don't want me in
there—" She pointed, eyes wide. "Oh, no! No, thank
you. No!"

"I do. Look, the births should be uncomplicated, but
you never know. We have to be prepared for anything.
We have two babies coming, and I want another pair
of hands to help me. Now, W.T. will be at Debra's head,
helping her follow my instructions. I don't think it's
appropriate for young Billy Joe to be in there, unless
we're desperate. And I want you to—"

"Neal—" She interrupted, squeezing his arm. "Neal,
I don't know. I've never done anything like this before.
When I agreed to come along, I didn't know you wanted
me to help deliver babies. That's not why I'm here in the
first place!"

He countered sharply. "Then why did you tag along?
Curiosity?"

"To help you."

"I need real help, not excuses! A woman is going to give birth to twins in there in a couple of hours. And those babies could be in danger if all of us don't do our jobs. I only have two hands. And I'll soon have three people who'll need attention. Can I depend on you, or do I have to get the sixteen-year-old?"

"Well, I..." Gwyn crumbled inside. She'd come along because Neal had said he needed her. Now it sounded as though she were trying to back out of the bargain. "I ... I'll try, Neal."

"Thank you." His expression gentled, and he set his coffee cup on the counter. Sandwiching her hands between his, he pulled her close. "It'll be the most rewarding thing you've ever done, Gwyn."

Neal's hands felt warm and strong and very capable. And she trusted him. "I don't know if I'll be much help, though. I'm nervous already."

"You can do this, Gwyn. I'll tell you exactly what to do. I'm not asking you to deliver the babies. I want you to help once they arrive. Just be there to assist. But I can't have you passing out. I don't need four patients, and one of them flat on the floor."

His strength seemed to transfer to her, filling her with a strange new confidence. She took a deep breath and smiled bravely. "Okay, Doctor. I'll help. And don't worry about me. I'm not the fainting type."

"Good." He kissed her quickly and squeezed her hands. "I knew I could count on you. I'll tell you what to do if you feel a little light-headed. Now, let's assemble the team. I have some specific instructions for each of you. And we have work to do to get ready for two babies."

They utilized the next hour and a half to drape the bed with clean sheets, move additional lamps into the room, prepare a table for the infants and go over details. Neal was wonderfully calm and precise, and his attitude spread to the others. Gwyn stood by Neal's side at the foot of the bed, watching anxiously as the first infant's tiny crown appeared.

"W.T., Debra," Neal said as he lifted the child. "You've got a little girl. She looks healthy."

Within seconds the baby's squeaky cry could be heard. Everyone in the room responded enthusiastically. Neal placed the tiny baby on Debra's tummy for a few minutes, so they could see her and the parent bonding could begin.

"She sounds good and strong," Neal said. "Looks like she's a fine, healthy baby!"

Fortunately there was a delay of about half an hour before the next birth. Gwyn helped Neal clean and stabilize the first tiny infant, then she wrapped the baby securely and placed her in the hand-made crib that had cradled four other Hancock babies. The next birth wasn't as speedy, but there were no problems. And soon they heard the second squeaky cry.

"Another gal!" Neal announced. "Do you hear her, Debra? She's a little spitfire. Probably hungry. And wants attention already!"

Everyone laughed with giddy relief as both babies' lusty cries filled the room. Debra smiled through her tears and caressed her new daughters, both tucked inside the crib by her bed. W.T. hugged his wife, then shook hands with Neal and Gwyn. His relief turned to pride and joy as he hovered over the infants. Eventually he brought out a bottle of homemade wine to toast the births, his wife, the doctor and his reluctant assistant.

After making sure his three patients were stable and resting, Neal decided it was all right to leave. He and Gwyn headed back down the mountain. The heavy rain had turned to intermittent mist; thick fog now made driving extremely hazardous, however.

"You were pretty terrific back there," Gwyn said with quiet admiration.

"You weren't so bad yourself, for a first timer." He glanced over at her, his blue eyes sincere. "I hope you'll forgive me for badgering you into helping. I felt a little desperate when I realized how inexperienced you and W.T. were. But I'm proud of you. Next time you'll know what to expect and—"

"Whoa! Hold it! I'm not planning on a 'next time.' I don't know if I'm cut out for being a doctor's assistant. I was so nervous!"

"It didn't show. I think you did well."

"I've never seen such tiny babies."

"Now you can add that you assisted the delivery of twins to your report. Your boss will be impressed, I'm sure."

"They'll never believe me back at the office!" She put her head back on the seat and laughed. "I can hardly believe it myself."

"You definitely left this place better than you found it, Ms Frederick," he said with a proud smile. "Two healthy babies and a happy family. You can't get much better than that."

She reached out and placed her hand over his on the steering wheel. "There's a rumor around here that you're a darn good physician, Dr. Perry. Some even go so far as to say you're the best they've seen. After tonight, and my keen observation all week, I'd have to agree."

"The best? That's a laugh! Delivering a baby is one thing. Saving lives quite another." His face tightened, his eyes stared straight ahead and the jubilant mood was broken.

Gwyn couldn't understand his sudden change, but she chalked it up to his being tired. The faint light of dawn was creeping into the misty-gray sky. They'd been up all night. She, too, was weary, although she was still functioning on the emotional high that followed the successful births of the twins. "It's been quite a night, Neal. I'm beginning to understand your devotion to your patients, even though it seems to take all your attention and energy."

"Now you can see why I'm used to functioning on a crisis level. I can't even have any real privacy. I'm sorry about our, uh, interruption. That was unfair." He continued to look straight ahead, his lips pressed together in a tight line.

"And inconvenient."

"I'm used to it." He shrugged. "Goes with the territory."

"Well, Doctor, what you need is someone to arrange a method of insulation to protect your privacy."

"Like?"

"I don't know. I'll have to work on that one." She glanced at him. "Especially since I am an interested party."

"Interested? That's nice to know."

"Well, I'm not one to leave something unfinished."

"Do I detect incentive?"

"Could be." She caressed the top of his hand with three fingertips. "But you were right about one thing, Neal."

"What's that?"

"There are real people who live on that mountain. And now two more." She squeezed his hand. "And I don't—can't really—complain about the night. There'll be other times for us."

"Hope so." He gave her a tight, grateful smile, pleased that she was capable of functioning beyond emotion. "Thanks, Gwyn. For helping and understanding."

She took his hand and pressed it to her lips for a kiss. "My pleasure, Neal."

THE UNMISTAKABLE ROAR of rushing water reached them before they rounded the curve and met the dangerously swollen Harmony Creek. In only a matter of hours the creek had risen to a point where driving through it was impossible. They both knew it. There was no need to discuss it. They were stranded.

Neal back up and parked the Jeep on high ground. "It'll be safe here, even if the creek rises more."

"You knew it would happen, didn't you?"

"I suspected it." He grabbed his black bag from the back seat, as well as the extra blanket she'd brought. "We had no choice but to cross it and go to the Hancocks'. But now we'll head for an alternate route."

"There's another bridge?"

"Well, it's not for vehicles. It's a footbridge."

"Then there actually is a bridge to somewhere?"

"You might say that. Here, use this to keep the rain off while we hike." He arranged the blanket like a shawl around her head and shoulders, then, in a lingering caress, trailed his thumbs along both her cheeks. "You're beautiful Gwyn," he murmured.

"Even with bloodshot eyes and dark moons under them?" She thought of all the times she'd tried to look good for him. A compliment was the last thing she'd expected from him now.

"Especially. Shows your strength of character." He stroked her lips and chin with his thumbs. "We share these bloodshot eyes. But they're for a good cause. Now, if we can just get home, we can get some rest and . . . who knows?"

She smiled. "What are we waiting for?"

They hiked a short distance through wet underbrush to a flimsy-looking structure spanning Harmony Creek. Neal proceeded. "This leads to the woods behind the clinic. We'll have quite a hike, but the route eventually leads home."

"Neal! You didn't say it was—" Gwyn hung back, her heart in her throat.

"A swinging bridge." He paused and glanced back. Her expression was one of alarm and fear. "It's made of steel cables, strong and sturdy." He shook the thing to prove it. An object flew through the mist to plunge into the rushing stream twenty feet below. "That was just a wooden slat. Everything's fine. Come on."

"No, everything's not fine." She stood her ground, even though it was starting to rain harder.

He came back to her and reached out. "I'll hold your hand. Come on."

"No." She kept her eyes on his face. "I think I'd rather wade across."

"That's ridiculous! Can't you see how fast that water's moving? It would sweep you away."

"All the way to the Tennessee River?"

"At least to the Ocoee."

"I'll take my chances."

"Gwyn, you aren't making sense. Can't you see—"

"No, I . . . I'll take your word for it." She took a step backward. She did not want to see anything. She knew only that bridge terrified her.

He stepped closer, his voice low and steady. "Gwyn, do you trust me?"

"Yes, of course, but—"

"Then listen to me. We'll hold on to each other. I won't let anything happen to you."

"That other thing fell."

"That was loose wood."

"I can't do this, Neal. You can see right through the floor."

"Keep your eyes on my face. And hold on. You can do it."

"No, I can't." She shook her head and lifted tearful eyes to him.

"You just wait." Quickly he unbuttoned his coat and unbuckled his belt. He hooked his physician's bag to the belt and buckled it again. "See? Both hands to hold you." He clasped each of her hands in his. "We'll walk like this." He took a step backward.

She took a step with him. "I'm so scared, Neal."

"Keep your eyes on mine," he said, moving onto the bridge. "Whatever you do, don't look down. Keep your head up."

She took each step along with him, keeping her head straight, her eyes up. They took another step, then another. The bridge jiggled, just as it was designed to do. She froze. "Oh, dear Lord, it's moving.'"

"Not much. This is—Don't look down!"

She gripped him with all her might, trying not to panic, trying to be a good sport. It was one of the hardest things she'd ever done, but with Neal's help she thought she could do it.

Inch by inch, step by step, they moved across the bridge. Neal repeated his constant low, steady-toned encouragement. Gwyn kept her eyes locked on his and breathed in gasps. They progressed, eyes mating, hands clasped, feet shuffling together, as if they were doing a stilted dance shrouded in the foggy mist.

Suddenly a gust of wind set the swinging bridge in motion, and Neal stumbled backward. He did a quick double step, trying to regain his balance, but Gwyn's weight pushed him back on his rear.

Gwyn screamed and fell onto him, clinging like a frantic wildcat. And the swinging bridge did what it did best. It took the action by swinging. And swinging.

Gwyn buried her face against his coat and muffled her sobs. She was in the middle of this bridge and couldn't go either way. So her only solution was to stay put.

Neal waited for a few minutes until her initial hysteria subsided and the wildly swinging bridge slowed down. "It's okay, Gwyn. Let's go again."

"No!"

He waited. They were in the middle of the bridge, in the midst of another cloudburst, and Gwyn wasn't about to hop up and continue the journey. She was finished, **had** gone as far as she could. But it was only halfway.

Neal sighed. There was nothing else to do. He struggled to his knees and lifted her in his arms. She clung desperately to him and the blanket sheltering her fell free. It floated, like a billowing parachute, down to the rushing stream beneath them. He was glad she didn't see it.

When they reached the other side, he set her down beneath a large blue spruce. The spreading branches provided a temporary shelter from the pouring rain. "Gwyn, you're safe." He pried her gripping hands from him and framed her face with his hands. "Gwyn, open your eyes. You're on solid ground."

She gazed up at him. His dark hair was slicked down on his forehead, large droplets clung to his eyebrows and beard and he looked awful. And wonderful! She didn't know when a man had ever looked more handsome to her! She smiled weakly, suddenly ashamed of her behavior. "I was pretty bad, wasn't I?"

"Not great."

"Sorry. I should have told you about my fear of heights."

"We didn't exactly discuss the subject."

"I'm sorry I was so much trouble."

"It's over now. You okay?"

She nodded, unable to stop shivering.

He pulled her to her feet. "Come on. Let's go home and get some sleep before my patients begin arriving."

As she followed Neal through the woods, Gwyn thought of Ed's initial promise regarding the SHARE program. Not for glory. What an understatement!

She was wet, cold and exhausted. But, crazily, she was glad to be on Neal's team. And she could hardly wait until she was again in his arms.

When they arrived home, Gwyn decided to take a shower. She stood under the warm spray, gratefully absorbing the heat into her chilled body. She washed her hair and dried it before leaving the heat-filled, steamed bathroom. Wrapped in a large white towel, she stepped into her room. It was cold and vacant. She gazed at the quilt-covered bed, relishing its warmth and the redeeming rest it offered. Yet deep inside she knew this wasn't where she belonged.

Turning her back on the room, she slowly walked down the hall and through the kitchen. She pushed Neal's door open and stood there for a minute, looking at him. He was already in bed, his dark hair gleaming with moisture from his recent shower.

Neal thought he was seeing an apparition, wrapped Indian-style in a white towel. But the apparition had thick, brunette hair and large, dark eyes, and appeared in the form of Gwyn. Heart pounding, he propped himself up on one elbow and stared at her. "Gwyn?"

"Neal. I don't want to be alone. Would you hold me?"

Immediately he turned back the quilted covers and silently extended one arm to her.

She dropped the towel and walked toward him.

7

LIKE A FANTASY out of the mists, she moved toward him. For a moment Neal wondered if he was dreaming, if the sight of her was a manifestation of his exhaustion. But she kept coming, a tiny smile on her lips. She reached the edge of the bed, and he caught a whiff of sweet honey and exotic, erotic spices. He inhaled deeply, craving more. The sensual scent of her proved he wasn't fantasizing—or crazy. She was real!

Her golden skin contrasted luxuriously with her curly mass of mahogany hair. Nude, she was even sexier than she had been in tights and leotard. Whoever said illusion was better than reality hadn't seen Gwyn's body.

Her bare shoulders sloped gracefully into slender arms that framed her high, firm breasts. The sight of her pert nipples circled by swollen, burgundy areolae was bewitching. Her trim waist tapered and seemed to be cinched by her tight, little navel. Feminine hips flared gently and extended into long straight legs. At the triangular juncture of those tempting thighs was a dangerously sexy patch of dark curls.

Dangerous, because Neal thought he would die if he couldn't touch that spot—and burst into a million pieces if he did. He swallowed and managed to mumble her name. "Gwyn. Come here."

Moving like silk, she slid into his open arms, and suddenly she was no longer a mystery. She was reality and warmth, beauty and desire. She was caring and sharing and loving. She was everything he had missed and needed. She was Gwyn. Her name was an aphrodisiac for him; her body a passionate seduction.

"Gwyn . . ." he whispered as he pressed her to him, and felt his passion grow stronger with each heat-filled moment. He wanted to shout and take her physically and completely. But he managed restraint. Barely managed.

Gwyn knew this was a bold move. In other circumstances, other times, she couldn't have done it. But this morning, with Neal, she couldn't help herself. "Did I disturb you?" She felt him tightly aroused as he wrapped himself around her.

"You have disturbed my every minute from the night you stepped into the clinic."

"I mean now," she murmured, quivering uncontrollably against him. The friction they created made a feverish heat.

"I can't sleep every night, thinking of you in there." He drew the covers over them. "You cold?"

She wriggled in his embrace. "I was when I was in there all alone. Then I thought you might be a good source of heat. Warm me up, Neal."

Neal almost laughed aloud with joy. "I'll make you warmer than you've ever been."

She chuckled softly. "Promise?"

"Mmm, I hope." Each minute of holding back increased the agony, until his whole body pulsated with uncontained male power. "Gwyn, this holding pattern can't last. Are you protected?'"

"I'm on the pill." She shifted to adjust their alignment, her softness to his hard. She was woman to his man, her shape molded to his as if proclaiming the awesome wonder of it and the promise of culmination. Her breasts sought the solid wall of his chest; her arms encircled his ribs; her hands clutched his back, pressing him to her. "I didn't come here just for holding."

"I want to touch you everywhere," he murmured, kissing her cheek, her earlobe, her neck. "I want you in every way, Gwyn." He rocked his pelvis forward, and her thighs parted slightly to accept the persistence of his maleness.

A pleasurable sigh caught in her throat. She'd wanted him, too. That was why she'd visited his room. But now that she was here, feeling him in the most intimate way, she wondered if she'd been too bold taking the first step. Now she could feel him large and strong against her, and she knew there was no turning back from this moment.

"Not having second thoughts, I hope."

"Do you read minds?"

"Bodies are my medium." He stroked the curve of her back and cupped both hands around the half-moon crescents of her hips.

"What does mine say?"

"Yours says 'don't stop now.'" Urged by the deep ache of desire, aroused, he thrust against her, pressing his fingers into the tight flesh of her buttocks.

"Yours says 'this woman never sleeps.'" She undulated with his pressure.

"No, no, you're misreading the signals. Mine says 'I can't believe my good fortune!'" With one hand he tilted her chin up for his kiss. "I couldn't sleep another night without you." His lips were soft and invitingly sensuous as they paired with hers, prying gently until his tongue could slip between them.

She parted her lips, inviting his further intrusion. With a seductive inward motion he sought the sweet warmth of her mouth. She countered by sparring with her tongue.

Gwyn heard a low groan and realized it was her own. She had never felt such strong urges and couldn't seem to get enough of his touch, of him. She was overwhelmed by everything about him and suddenly knew she had to have him in her. Mere holding was no longer satisfying. She wanted to hold him ultimately in the closest possible way. His caressing only fueled the fire growing inside her. She had to touch him, to know every part of him completely, to share their bodies.

His hand cascaded down her form, pausing at the base of her throat, lingering to caress the twin swollen mounds braced on his chest. She arched at his touch, then quivered as his fingers trailed down her middle and pressed into the soft warmth of her femininity. She thought she'd die.

He pushed her legs apart. "Gwyn, I can't wait. Have to have you."

"Me, too." She placed her hand on him and gently squeezed.

He slid over her, stretching himself with her, wedging between her thighs. He kissed her, breathing her name in a plea.

"Yes, yes." She tilted her pelvis upward and guided him into her. His masculine arousal throbbed inside her, setting her on fire, igniting the flames already smoldering within her. She wanted him as much as he wanted her, and they merged with hard, matching thrusts. In a flashing, intense passion they became one. Their union felt right. How could she have doubted it?

Gwyn couldn't believe the wellspring of emotion that accompanied the frenzied physical act. She was with him every moment, meeting his thrusts, matching his low moans, feeling as he felt.

She lost all sense of time and place; her desire for ultimate fulfillment had taken over her entire being. He couldn't reach deeply enough into her, couldn't take enough of her giving. When he exploded into her, she exulted in his gratification. Then she was undulating, faster and harder, crying his name softly, over and over. And when she reached her climax, her consciousness tumbled in a frenzy of physical and emotional joy.

Her passion surrounded him, evolving into tender affection. She never wanted to give him up, never wanted to leave this warm place where she'd found such ecstasy. Slowly she returned to the reality of their two bodies still clinched, her consciousness weaving into the euphoric aftermath of ultimate pleasure. "Neal..." she murmured.

"Hmm?" He nuzzled her ear.

"Do you mind?"

"Mind what?"

"That I came to you."

"It was exciting. I wanted you here, Gwyn. This is where you belong."

"Seems that way, doesn't it?" She stroked his back, spreading her fingers across its width, trying to absorb him into her fingertips. "Would you have come to me?"

"Not this morning." He felt her almost imperceptible wince. "But it would have happened eventually. It was inevitable. I couldn't have held out much longer." He tugged her earlobe with gentle teeth.

"I'm glad I came," she said with a giggle.

"Me, too. I was worried about you coming." He trailed his kisses across her cheek to her lips. "But only for a minute."

"I meant—"

"I know what you meant." He chuckled. "And I'm glad we both came." His kiss sealed her lips for another prolonged, sensuous moment. When he raised his head, his voice was gravelly. "We were better than I dreamed we would be." He kissed a warm spot on her neck. "And I've dreamed about you since the day we met."

"You have?" She wriggled with pleasure.

"Hmm, you dominate my thoughts. And now my body. Completely."

They clung as long as possible, finally slipping apart to nestle together like two birds in a storm. And they dozed.

GWYN AWOKE AFTER NOON. The full gravity of what she'd done came over her. She'd given herself, wantonly, to a man she hardly knew. To a client. What would Ed do if he knew? Probably fire her for such an indiscretion. A part of her said she'd slipped, made a mistake. This encounter never should have happened. And it wouldn't have, either, if she hadn't been the one to initiate it. At least, not last night. How could she have been so weak?

She stared wonderingly at the dark-haired man sleeping beside her. He was so strong and handsome; no wonder she'd fallen for his masculine charms. She admired his disheveled dark hair and decided he wore his magnificent beard like a proud Viking warrior. And yet she didn't think a gentler man existed.

He was altogether different from any man she'd ever known. Maybe it was that marked difference that had intrigued her and lured her into his bed. Her romantic nature had swayed her ability to think and act within reason.

Neal shifted, trapping her with one outflung arm. She examined his muscular arm, sprinkled generously with dark, curly hairs down to the tops of his skillful hands, each long finger bearing a dark tuft— Heavens! What was wrong with her, mentally raving like this? Reasons didn't matter! She had to start thinking straight.

Neal is merely an interesting man who intrigued you and caught your fancy, she told herself. But her little voice added, *Neal is a marvelous man who makes you feel like none other.* She had to agree with that reasoning. Neal alerted her senses, appealed to the feminine part of her and made her feel as special and wanted as he was.

That was it!

Neal Perry was a very special man, partly because he was a much-beloved physician, partly because he was a man who knew how to love her. And she was infatuated with that man, much as a patient might become enamored with a doctor who had saved her life. It was an old trick of the emotions.

Reality was, though, that she relished every moment of being with him, whether it was helping him with patients, sparring over time schedules or making love. Heavens! How he could love her!

She stifled a shudder as she remembered the special moments of their early-morning love fest. How could she ever think of him as an ordinary man? He was magnificent. And she was vulnerable to his attraction.

Since coming to Harmony Creek, she'd been confronted with stronger, deeper feelings than she'd ever known. Her involvement with Neal seemed to be inevitable, uncontrollable. She was overwhelmed with an abiding respect for him, but also a great fondness, a tenderness for the man and his personal needs. Was that love?

Was it possible—she tingled all over at the thought—that love was what she was feeling with Neal? No, it couldn't be. It was too soon. And they were too different. Anyway, she'd be leaving here in another week. She'd go back to Chicago as if nothing had ever happened between her and Neal.

The thought drove her crazy. She should end it now, before things became more complicated. She felt Neal's hand move, and froze, tingling even more.

Gwyn peeked at his face. The man beside her appeared asleep, with eyes closed and a contented expression. But his hand now cupped her breast, as surely as if it belonged there.

"I would have gone in there for you," a sleepy, masculine voice muttered. His fingers moved and gently massaged her breast. "I wouldn't have let you get away."

She felt a rush of warmth at his caress, his voice teasing her. "You have to say that now," she whispered.

His hand grew firm on her breast as he pressed his palm against her tight nipple. "I would have gone after you, flung you over my shoulder and carried you into my lair."

"Sounds exciting."

"Very." He scooted closer. "I get excited . . . just thinking about you. This—" he threw one leg over hers, taunting her with his hot male arousal "—was happening too often. I couldn't sleep without you."

Gwyn caught her breath. Neal was purposely tempting her, just as she'd tempted him last night. She grew tight inside, knowing that he wanted her and thinking about making love to him again.

"There's only one thing to do about this, uh, little problem of mine. You have tremendous power over me, Gwyn. Your sexy body has captured me completely. And only you can release me."

Her heart pounded, and her body flushed with sudden heat as he moved closer. She couldn't escape. Furthermore, she didn't want to. She was being taken in by his charms again, by his strong sexuality challenging—arousing—hers. She tried to protest. "Neal, we need—"

His kiss halted her. "We need each other. Can't you feel it?" His hand touched her face, fingertips caressing and stroking every inch. "Mmm, just as I remember." He began kissing the places he'd stroked, her eyelids, her temples, her cheeks, her chin, her mouth. His tongue edged her lips and slipped inside for a taste of her honey.

She thought about telling him of her decision. To end it now. To never tell anyone. But his kiss, and her reaction, caught her off guard. She decided to wait until her mouth wasn't so busy. The next thing she knew, his lips were caressing her breasts, switching from one to the other, brushing her sensitive skin with bristled kisses, taking her nipples into his mouth. Oh, if she died now, she'd be in ecstasy!

She gripped his shoulders, trying to catch her breath as his lips made moist trails down her middle. She'd have to tell him later. Much later. She couldn't deny herself Neal's pleasures one more time. She was too weak willed.

She gasped aloud when he reached the curly mound of femininity and sought her tight bud of delight. He knew what to do to make her respond like a sensuous woman. And she couldn't help herself.

As Neal hovered over her, giving her pleasures she'd never dreamed of, Gwyn knew she was making excuses to herself. She wanted him as much as he did her. Maybe more. Maybe it was all right to admit to passion. This once.

"Relax, Gwyn. I want to kiss you . . . everywhere."

"I—" She paused as his lips trailed along her inner thigh. "I'm trying to, but—"

"I can feel your hesitation at what's happening. Your tension. But your responses to me are strong. They match mine."

"I feel like we're out of control."

"Let me do this. Out of your control." He lowered himself to her. Erotically he pleasured her with his lips until she quivered all over with pulsing sensations.

"Don't stop," she moaned as his kisses brought her to the brink of passion. "Ohhh . . . this can't be wrong, Neal. It feels too wonderful."

"It isn't wrong, Gwyn." He made a moist trail with his tongue down her middle. "It's too good." He touched the throbbing mound of her sweet, hot femininity.

She shuddered beneath his sensuous strokes and began a steady climb to ultimate bliss. With each motion she writhed and arched, her desire building in intensity and strength beyond her control. Her climax came in multiple ripples that surged through her body again and again until she thought—wished—they would never stop.

Finally she breathed a low moan, and he joined her for another ride, this one hard and fast. He drove into her, thrusting deeply, and she responded with a sexual reawakening. Amazingly, the second time was as intense as the first.

They dozed and woke later. Curled together, they lay with his arm around her shoulders, her head on his chest. To Neal, it seemed perfectly natural. He'd missed this. Not the sex so much as the warmth and intimacy. Missed having a woman, like Gwyn, who cared and wanted to please him. Maybe he'd been wrong all along. Withdrawal wasn't the answer. Gwyn was. His arm tightened around her.

She noticed in his slight movement a change from the slow swell and dip of his chest in sleep. He felt wonderful, holding her like this. She inhaled his masculine scent, now mingled with the musky odors of their lovemaking. Running her fingers through the dark, curly mat of hair beneath her head, she rubbed one beaded nipple. She loved listening to the regular rhythm of his heart, loved to rub his taut muscles. There was an earthy appeal about him that she couldn't deny. Or resist. But she must.

"Gwyn . . . Gwyn . . ." He said her name with a sigh. "This has been heaven. You are so sexy. . . ."

"We really shouldn't let our lust take over like this."

"Why? I thought we were pretty good together."

"We were, but . . ." She tried to push herself away.

He held her tightly and nuzzled the area beneath her ear. "I'm glad you came," he murmured with a chuckle.

She smothered a giggling response. "Please, don't—"

"What's wrong?"

"I don't do this sort of thing lightly, Neal."

"Neither do I. But I must say, we—"

"Please!" She pushed herself away from him this time and lay back on the pillow, her hand on her forehead. "Please, Neal, we have to put an end to this now. Before it goes any further!"

"Why? How much further can we go?"

"Don't joke. We both have too much at stake." She lay quivering on the pillow next to him.

He propped himself up on one elbow and hovered over her. "You mean, *you* have too much at stake?"

She nodded. "Well, I do. My career . . . my—"

Neal gaped at her, his blue eyes hard. "Your job in Chicago."

"Yeah."

With a groan he rolled away and sat on the edge of the bed with his back to her.

Gwyn was in agony as she puzzled over the predicament she'd created. She was confused with her own jumbled feelings, and she'd made Neal angry. She couldn't blame him. After a night—morning, actually—of wild lovemaking, she was calling it quits. Privately she knew that she'd enjoyed the experience far too much. And it scared her.

A part of her wanted to stay here forever. Another more rational part reminded her of the inherent problems with that thought. "Please, Neal, try to look at this from a realistic perspective. We both have very different things to do."

Neal stood and slowly turned around to face her in all his nude male glory. "Do feelings enter into this? Don't you *feel* anything?"

"Of course." She sucked in her breath, incapable of

answering further at the moment. All she could do was admire.

The man was magnificent, standing before her with legs spread and arms akimbo! She'd felt the strength of that broad chest, the tickle of those dark curls that rambled down his middle to encircle his proud manhood. And she'd felt that male power, that ultimate passion of a man for a woman. And she'd known her own sexual fulfillment with him. Gwyn stared at him, transfixed and speechless, but the admiration in her eyes gave her feelings away.

In one swift movement he propped one knee on the bed, reached for her shoulders and hauled her against him for a lengthy kiss that left her heart pounding and her limbs shaky. He was impossible to resist, and she clung weakly to his bare, lean waist.

"Neal, don't do this," she begged.

He looked into her eyes. "Didn't you like it, Gwyn?"

"I...I..."

"Can you answer that honestly?"

His lips were dangerously close to hers, and she found breathing difficult. She wanted to kiss him herself, to pull him back down on the bed—but she had to gain control of herself! "Yes. Any woman would."

He shook his head. "I wouldn't kiss any woman like that, Gwyn. Only you. But don't worry. I won't do it again without your permission. Or just put me down on your schedule."

"Neal, we let our lust take over our reason."

"Is that what you think?"

She nodded.

His eyes narrowed. "I disagree. If I just wanted to satisfy my libido, I could have had a woman—any woman. You're the only one I've felt anything beyond passion for in two years. To me, that's something special. To you . . . I guess it's just raw sex."

Raw sex? Oh, yes! The words were exciting. Gwyn swayed against his leg and tried not to think of his nude body so close to hers. "Neal, I . . . I didn't mean it that way. You *are* special. Like no one I've ever known."

"After what we've shared, can you honestly say you felt nothing beyond desire?"

"No." She lifted her face to him, silently begging for a kiss.

Instead he released her and stepped away, folding his arms across his chest. "Case dismissed!"

Nude, she slumped in the middle of the bed, looking up at him beseechingly. "But that's not the whole case," she insisted. "There's more than just us."

"What about something spontaneous and beautiful between two people? Doesn't that count for something?" He turned toward the bathroom.

"Neal?" She shivered and pulled the top quilt around her shoulders.

He halted and looked back at her. She was gorgeous, sitting in the middle of his bed, wrapped in a colorful quilt, mahogany hair tousled sexily. It was a picture he'd remember long after she was gone. And that's what she was trying to tell him, that in another week she'd be gone. He knew she was trying to make the break easier on both of them. But he didn't want to face the end just when they'd gotten started.

She smiled, that sexy, little Mona Lisa smile that drove him crazy. "We were rather good together, weren't we?"

He straightened and took a breath. Light danced in her chocolate eyes, and he could see the joy she was trying to hide. His heart leaped with hope. Maybe all wasn't lost, after all. "We were great, Gwyn."

While he was in the shower, she slipped into her room to shower and dress. When she emerged, he was sipping hot coffee at the table.

"I've had a chance to think about it, Neal. I haven't changed my mind," she said as she poured herself a cup. "It's for the best if we keep our distance."

He looked up at her, an expression of anger filling his blue eyes. "Can't you do something that isn't planned, just once, Gwyn?"

She whirled around, her dark eyes snapping. "What happened this morning wasn't planned. It was about as spontaneous as possible. And I initiated it! But that doesn't change the total picture."

"Does everything—even feelings—have to fit into your damned scheme of things?" He stalked out of the room.

She stared bleakly after him.

They spent the remainder of the day in silent misery, doing Saturday duties. Housecleaning and laundry occupied their time and kept them apart. Neal had a few patients in the afternoon, and later Gwyn helped him clean the office. By evening the previous night's loss of sleep had caught up with them, and they were both tired. They ate an uninspired dinner of baked chicken and rice by the fire and turned in early.

THE NEXT DAY wasn't much better. Neal announced he was going back to Buck Mountain to check on Debra and the twins. It was understood he'd have to hike back across that swinging bridge to get to the Jeep, so he didn't even ask if she wanted to go along. Gwyn certainly didn't volunteer.

While he was gone, she read a magazine and ironed

her clothes for the week and finally, in complete boredom—or was it frustration?—went for a walk. When she returned, Neal was in the kitchen, cooking.

"How're Debra and the twins?"

"Fine. She's a strong woman. And the kids seem to be healthy, which is a good thing. I'm not sure how I'd get her to a hospital with the roads like this. The creek is still too high to ford."

"What are you making?"

"My Sunday night special. Frozen pizza." He pulled the pan from the oven.

She eyed the fare skeptically but withheld comment.

He read her expression. "Don't you like pizza?"

"Oh, yes. The kind with real crust and real cheese."

"This one has all that." He took a bite. "Not bad."

"If you like tomato sauce on cardboard."

"You can do better?"

"The pizza shop can do better."

"Well, there happens not to be a pizza shop within fifty miles. And they charge extra for delivery out here!"

She glared at him.

He glared at her.

She looked down. "I'm sorry, Neal. You're right. This is ridiculous. In a pinch, frozen pizza will do."

"I don't think it's pizza that we're arguing about here."

She pressed her lips together and nodded. "I know. We're both a little tense."

After a few minutes of silence he said, "I have something nice to tell you. Maybe it'll ease the tension between us."

"Oh?"

"Debra and W.T. have decided on names for the babies. One will be Elizabéth Gwyn after you and their paternal grandmother. The other will be Amanda Nell for Debra's mother and me. I guess Nell is pretty close to Neal."

Suddenly Gwyn's eyes filled with tears. "I've never had a child named after me. How endearing. I feel so—" She halted as emotions choked her. She pressed fingers to her lips.

"It's a nice gesture, since you helped deliver them."

"Oh, I did nothing! You were the one."

He shook his head. "But you were there and didn't shirk from what needed to be done. You came along and helped bring two babies into the world. That's a wonderful feeling, Gwyn."

"Yes, it is." She smiled and happy tears glistened in her dark eyes.

"The Hancocks are very grateful for what you did." He looked at her sincerely. "And so am I. We, uh, could have lost one or both babies. I needed you there with me."

"It was an experience I'll never forget, Neal." She shook her head and clasped her hands together. "I can't believe it. Not even my brother named either of his daughters after me."

"There'll be a little Gwyn growing up on Buck Mountain with her sister, Nell." Spontaneously he reached out and took her hands. Gently he pulled her close into a hug. "I'd say you're going to leave quite a legacy around here, Gwyn Frederick."

She laughed softly and placed her hands on his chest, relishing the strength she found there. "Wait'll they hear about this at the office! Now I have a baby named after me!" She leaned her head toward him, resting it on his shoulder. "Oh, Neal, this whole experience has been wonderful. I can't believe how good I feel when I'm with . . . when I'm here."

"Do you realize what you're saying, Gwyn?"

She lifted her head, her dark eyes meeting his with stark recognition. "No, I don't," she whispered. "We can't let this happen again, Neal."

"Is that what you really want, Gwyn?"

Before she could answer, the phone rang. It was a blaring intrusion into their privacy. After two days of uncomfortable silence between them, they were just barely beginning to bridge the gap. Their world seemed to be one of constant interruptions. And now that they were communicating again, here was another interruption. Gwyn sighed heavily.

"Damn," Neal muttered as he moved away from her to answer it.

His shortness with the caller made her look up. He wouldn't talk that way to a patient. "For you," he mouthed.

Knowing instinctively who was on the line, she took the phone. "Travis. Hi."

"I've been trying to get you for two days. Where the hell have you been?"

Sleeping with the client, her mind screamed. Her guilty gaze met Neal's. "We've, uh, had several emergencies, Trav. But it's too complicated to explain now. I'll tell you all about it next week."

Neal walked away. Suddenly he was filled with an uncontrollable rage. She would be leaving soon, and the frustration he felt at the inevitable was almost overwhelming. He could even admit to a deeper pain. He wanted to yell, to rip that phone from the wall, to do something outrageous!

He had to get control of himself. Violence wasn't a

part of his makeup, but he surely felt vicious right now. He couldn't listen to her conversation for another minute, couldn't even stay cooped up within these walls. He tore a sheet from a prescription pad lying nearby, jotted down a few words and left the note on the table.

Gwyn watched, distracted from her conversation with Travis, as Neal's behavior turned bizarre. She was curious when he left the house so quickly. Her gaze fell on the paper he'd left on the table, and she strained to read it, stretching the telephone cord to its limit. But the note was too far away. She'd have to wait until she could hang up the phone.

Her curiosity obsessed her. Why had Neal looked so strange? Where had he gone? What had happened to make him behave so strangely?

"Gwyn, are you there?"

"Yes. Something's come up, Travis. I have to go. Talk to you next week when we both have more time." She hung up, then glared at the phone. What in the world was she doing? She'd cut Travis off with virtually no explanation. He'd be curious about her strange behavior. But right now she only cared about Neal.

She hurried over to the table and read his note: *I had the sudden impulse to jog!* She threw the note down and ran into her bedroom, grabbing a sweater and jerking on her jogging shoes with feverish, nervous hands. Without thinking of anything but finding him, she ran out of the house. It had started to rain again.

She dashed through the trees, hoping he'd gone to the woods, where he usually jogged. Storm clouds darkened the path; the rain made it sloppy. But still she ran on. Finally she saw him up ahead, taking the left fork in the path. "Neal! Wait up!"

He was panting, leaning one arm on a tree when she

reached him. "What do you want?" His voice was almost a growl, so different from the way he'd been speaking just before the phone rang.

She was breathing hard, too. What did she want? She wanted to reach out to him, to touch his face. Yet she couldn't move.

Rain pelted them as they faced each other in glaring silence.

"I want . . ." She halted, not knowing where to begin or what to say.

He was no help. He merely stood there, a stony expression on his face.

"I thought I could just shut you off, Neal. Just end things. But I—" she swallowed "—but I can't. These two days have been awful."

He shook his head. "I can't play your games, Gwyn. On again, off again isn't my style."

"Mine, either." She stepped forward and framed his face with her hands. "What I want, Neal, is you." She stood on tiptoe and kissed his rain-wet lips. They were surprisingly warm. But the rain made his skin cold.

Immediately Neal's arms swept around her. "Does this mean you're giving in to the urge to be spontaneous?" he asked when she finally lifted her lips.

"Spontaneous sounds wonderful," she said with a smile. "I haven't made a list in days."

He pulled her closer and dipped his head for another kiss. "Gwyn . . . Gwyn . . ."

"But I do have an agenda for the night," she murmured between kisses. "It requires a warm, dry bed. And two hot bodies."

"I'm sure that can be arranged. Race you home!" He

grabbed her hand.

They took off through the woods, their laughter echoing through the trees.

8

"HERE'S TO BABY Elizabeth Gwyn." Neal raised his wineglass.

"To little Amanda Nell." Gwyn lifted her glass to his. "And to their fine doctor."

"And to their doctor's brave assistant." Neal sipped his wine, then placed a Chardonnay-flavored kiss on her lips. "Hmm, you know what I like best about you?"

She returned the kiss. "I figure it's because I turn you on."

"That, too," he said with a chuckle. "Also, you come through with flying colors in a pinch."

"You taught me everything I know." She touched his face affectionately, letting her fingers explore the angular lines and burrow through the bristles of his beard.

"Not quite everything. You taught me about schedules, logs and multiple systems, and how time wasters are controlling my life." He set his glass down and reached for a sandwich triangle, dangling it under her nose. "Plus you brought nutrition back into my life. I'll be ever grateful."

"Grilled cheese sandwiches are probably not very high on the good-for-you list." She licked the melted cheese oozing from the edge of her sandwich. "But they are very satisfying."

"Much better than tomato sauce on frozen cardboard." He settled beside her on the sofa they'd pulled closer to the fireplace. "Ahh, this is nice. I don't know how I managed before you came into my life, Gwyn. Not very well, that's how!"

"Oh, you were doing just fine. Working too hard, leaving no time for play, and your time management stunk." She paused, then added, "And your sweet tooth had taken over your life. In spite of all that, you managed to be an excellent doctor."

"Now, thanks to you, I'm thinking about protein and Vitamin C."

"Not much, you aren't." She nibbled her sandwich. "But you do seem more in charge of your time. Except, of course, for the ever-present, unexpected crisis."

"I'm trying to change my ways. My patients just won't comply."

"They're learning, though."

"So am I." He slipped one arm around her shoulders, his hand caressing her hair, which was still damp from the rain. "Before you arrived, my life was a skeleton, an extremely lonely existence. Now you provide one constant, unexpected pleasure after another."

"You, lonely? I've never seen anyone more surrounded by people! Or so responsive to their most crucial needs. Yours is a workaholic existence, Doctor." She finished her sandwich and snuggled her head into his shoulder. "But I do admire your dedication to your profession."

"My dedication is to my patients. At one point I nearly threw my lofty profession away."

"You?" She sat up and looked at him. "Why?"

He took a sip of wine. "Disillusionment, mostly." He caressed her hair as if relishing its soft touch. Was it true to sum up his near ruination in that one word? Still, it was a comprehensive word that most reflected his view of everything at that time. "I was totally disillusioned with life and especially with the limitations of my abilities."

"I can't believe you almost quit being a doctor."

"Came very close."

"That would have been a great tragedy. Look at all the good you do, Neal."

He shrugged.

"What changed your mind?"

"A friend in med school. One of the guys in that photo by the phone. He said something sappy about throwing away my life and my ability to heal and my oath of commitment. Then he reminded me that my skills were severely limited outside the medical field. I needed a job." Neal paused for another sip of wine. "And he persuaded me to take this one until I could get my head on straight."

"What a good friend." Gwyn nestled her head on his chest again. "So being here salvaged your career?"

"Being almost constantly busy works wonders on a sick spirit. You don't have time to stew about disillusionment. Or anything else." He stroked her nape beneath her heavy, dark curls. "And being out here all alone, with no friends or relatives, I came face-to-face with myself. I had to decide whether or not to go on. Then how to go about that."

"Are you still disillusioned?"

He hesitated before answering. "No. I think I've reconciled with my past. And time has helped."

"This was recent, then?"

"Sometimes it seems like yesterday, sometimes like a lifetime ago." He sighed heavily and leaned his head back. "Yeah. I struggled through the last year of my residency, and when it was over, I applied for the opening here. I arrived last June."

"Was this after your fiancée's death?"

He paused. "Yep. Losing Maria made me a bitter physician. I failed at the most important job I ever had. Saving her life. And I couldn't deal with that."

Gwyn slipped her hand inside the button placket of his sweater, seeking the sensual warmth of his flesh, giving him her quiet affection. She pressed her palm to his heart. The beat was sure and strong. Slowly he was revealing the depth of his feelings regarding the tragedy that obviously changed the course of his life. Now she understood more.

"I'm sorry about your tragedy, Neal," she said softly, hoping he could tell that she really cared. "You're one of the strongest people I know. Strong and gentle and loving. I don't know anyone who's more dedicated. The people of Harmony Creek are very lucky to have you."

"And I'm lucky to have them. They've taught me a lot about life. And about love."

She pressed a kiss to his chest. "What could they possibly teach you about love?"

"I know that commitment without love doesn't work because it becomes an obligation. And love without commitment is empty because then it's selfish. They go hand in hand." He bent to kiss her curly crown.

"Do you think you could love again, Neal?"

He didn't answer right away. "I hope so."

She turned her face up to his and murmured softly. "Kiss me, Neal. Please..."

He pressed his lips to hers for a long, sensuous kiss.

"I've learned a little about love while I've been here, too," she whispered when the contact was finally broken. "That it can be more than male-female games. Your patients really love you. I can see it in their faces. And whether you realize it or not, you return that love in your dedication. Look at all you did to deliver Debra's babies."

He shrugged. "It's all I know." He kissed her forehead. "But you showed your true colors by going along. And helping."

"I know that what we've shared is the most wonderful experience I've ever had." She arched to press another kiss to his lips.

"My, my, you have learned a lot in a week." He shifted so they could face each other.

"I'm a quick study." She watched his blue eyes grow darker with renewed passion and felt drawn in to their alluring magic.

"I like the organized, efficient Gwyn," he began as he touched her face and hair randomly, reaffirming their silky textures with his fingertips. "She's smart and gets things done. But you know something crazy? I like the free-spirited Gwyn even better. I'm intrigued with the woman who came to my bed at dawn and made love to me in the early-morning hours."

"That's a completely different side of me," she admitted with a shy grin. "One that I'm just now learning about."

"That one just about drives me crazy." He trailed his finger down her nose and pressed it to her lips. "Be daring, Gwyn. Abandon yourself. Let it happen spontaneously between us."

"I'm afraid it's already happening, Neal." She could feel herself rapidly sinking into his appealing quicksand. "I've never felt this way with any man. So . . . so out of control."

"Give up the control. Let it take you—take us both— far away." His finger trailed down the front of her sweater.

"Sounds like a heavenly trip."

"To the top."

She gazed into his eyes. They promised the journey to the summit that she craved. Smiling with a devilish intention, she sat up and quickly pulled her sweater over her head and dropped it on the floor. She was nude underneath. "I'll let go if you will," she challenged.

He accepted her challenge with a roguish grin and pulled his sweater off, too.

"Oooh, I like." She ran her hands over his chest.

He cupped and lifted her breasts to his lips for a series of sweet, moist kisses. "Tempt me again," he demanded, his breath hot against her skin.

With a sexy smile on her rosy lips, she reached down to pull off her heavy socks and discard them with bawdy motions.

He eyed her skeptically. "You tease! Socks don't count! Take it all off!"

She eyed him up and down, then stood and turned her back to him. With a few seductive hip motions she slid her jogging pants down to her ankles and stepped out of them. When she turned around, he applauded and laughed aloud. "Great! My, my, when you let loose, you really let loose."

She folded her arms beneath her breasts, pushing them up tauntingly. "Okay. Now you let loose. It's only fair."

He stared at her, standing in the nude, her creamy flesh backlit by the fire. She was fabulous, and he was already feeling the effects of arousal from their erotic sex play. He pushed himself to his feet and, with his eyes glued to hers, stepped out of his pants.

Gwyn's traitorous eyes scanned his tall frame as he stood before her in all his magnificently aroused glory.

With a smile of pure delight she moved into his arms. "Sure is a nice body," she cooed, wriggling against him. "Fits mine in all the right places."

"I never thought I'd find a woman's body so beautiful and sexy as yours, Gwyn." He stroked her back all the way to her buttocks. "I can't get enough of you."

"Good." She shivered in eager anticipation and turned her head so she could press her ear to his chest. The strong throbbing of his heartbeat reverberated through her, creating a heated passion that grew in intensity. How could she have decided they didn't belong together? Being with him made her feel vibrant, but touching him like this hurled her into another dimension. They belonged together. Like this. She didn't know how they'd manage, but they would. This was too good to give up.

She turned her face up to kiss him. The kiss deepened as they drank hungrily from the sweetness each offered. He thrilled her with his obvious desire for her. As he moved to kiss her breasts, tantalizing her with erotic strokes of his tongue, she tingled all over with excitement. Taking each taut nipple gently between his teeth, he tugged, then laved each with his sensuous tongue. As his kisses continued to seek sensitive, erotic places on her body, she grew weak-kneed with desire.

When he knelt before her, she thought she'd crumble. Gripping his shoulders for support, she moaned her pleasure and trembled as his caresses became more intimate, more intense. With a low whimper she called his name as her knees buckled and she tumbled into his arms. "Oh, Neal!"

"Come here, Gwyn." He lay back on the sofa and pulled her over him. "You're a wild seductress!"

"You—" she paused to touch him "—bring out the best in me." His throbbing flesh quivered beneath her fingertips, and she stroked him softly.

"You...can't keep doing that," he muttered hoarsely.

"How about this?" She moved over him and braced her knees beside his hips. With a pleasurable smile she slowly lowered herself until they merged completely.

"Now that's more like it." His voice was a low groan.

Gwyn took a great deal of delight in watching his face as she worked her sensual magic. With palms on his chest she sat upright, forcing him deep inside her. "Now I have you where I want you!" She smiled down at him.

His hands rested on her thighs, his thumbs pressed on the center of her femininity. "Do you like the feeling of superiority?"

"I like this feeling," she murmured, lowering her chest to his. Her hips moved up and down, slowly at first, then with greater speed. Vigorously she rode him to the summit. Feelings and emotions blended and tumbled into a wildly raging passion. They clung together and let time take them, slowly, back to reality.

"Gwyn," he said finally.

"Hmm?"

"I think I'm falling..."

"Me, too." Her heart pounded. Could he be talking about love? Was that what she was feeling? Her feelings were so mixed up right now that she wanted answers.

"I'm going off the sofa." There was a light tone in his voice. She felt a jolt when his foot hit the floor as he tried to balance them.

Her heart plunged. He wasn't thinking of love. And she was being presumptuous. Did she think love would solve their predicament? That would probably make things worse. "I'm going with you, Neal."

"Then let's go to bed."

"Yes," she agreed, forgetting about everything but making love with him.

"WHERE'S THE DOC? I've got to see him right away!"

Gwyn looked up to see Mae entering the office in a huff the next morning. "He's with a patient now, but he'll be finished in a few minutes. What's wrong, Mae? Jed's hand isn't infected, is it?"

"No, Jed's fine as frog's hair. I'm the one in a snit! Just take a look at this!" She spread a newspaper on the desk and slapped the editorial page. "Who do those city slickers think they are, telling everybody we don't need that bridge!"

Gwyn read the article blasting the use of the federal flood monies for "the bridge to nowhere." She pressed her lips together and looked at Mae determinedly. "Well, maybe it's time we let them know that bridge *does* lead somewhere. And there are lots of families who need it."

Several patients clustered curiously around the desk, and Mae passed the newspaper to them. "I think Gwyn's right. It's time to take action."

"Neal, er, Dr. Perry, had to leave his Jeep on the other side of the creek after he went up on Buck Mountain Friday night," Gwyn said.

"Did Debra have her twins?" Mae asked quickly.

"Yes, both are girls."

"Hallelujah! Girls!" Mae smiled broadly. "How are they doing?"

"Everybody's great. Those babies are beautiful and so tiny, Mae, it's a miracle they're alive."

"Without our fine doc they might not be," Mae declared. "Or what if the creek had risen the night before they were born, and he couldn't have gotten up there in time?"

One of the men waiting to see the doctor spoke up. "I just came from the mountain this morning, and you still can't get across. I had to leave my truck where the doc parked his Jeep and walk."

"Across the swinging bridge?" Gwyn shivered at the thought.

"Yep. There's no other way."

Gwyn looked at Mae. "There's no other way. I think it's time for petitions. That's our next step to show the strength of our convictions."

Mae nodded emphatically. "That's why I'm here. I'm looking for support."

Neal appeared in the doorway of the waiting room. "You'll always get our support, Mae. What are you up to now?"

"Great! I knew I could count on you, Doc. I'm having a meeting at my house tonight to explain about the petitions and distribute them. Would you all come?"

Everyone in the room agreed with rowdy enthusiasm.

"Okay, tell everybody who wants a part in this to come on over tonight about seven," Mae said. Then she turned to the man from Buck Mountain. "If you'll stop by my house before you head back up the mountain, I'll give you some stew to take to the Hancocks."

"Will you save a little for a poor, starving doctor?" Neal asked with a grin.

"For you, Doc, anything! If you'll come to the meeting."

"I . . ." He glanced at Gwyn. "We'll be there. Corn bread, too?" he persisted with a grin.

"Of course." She smiled with obvious pride that the doctor had made a special request for her food. "If you'll take a page of the petition and fill it with signatures."

"You drive a hard bargain, Mae. But you're on. Leave it at the desk." He disappeared into the next examining room.

A new light glistened in Gwyn's eyes. "This clinic would be an excellent place to gather signatures, Mae. So many people come through here, and I'm sure most of them are in favor of building that bridge. It wouldn't take any time to fill a page. Leave several."

"You've changed your mind about the bridge, I take it?"

Gwyn nodded. "I went along with Dr. Perry the night the Hancock twins were born. I saw that raging creek for myself. And the trouble it causes. Anyway—" she paused with a little smile "—now that I have a namesake on the mountain, I feel it's my duty to make life better for her."

"They named one of the twins after you?"

"Elizabeth Gwyn. Isn't that beautiful? The other one is Amanda Nell for the doctor who delivered them both safely. And the grandmothers of both babies, Elizabeth and Amanda."

"Fancy that." Mae beamed. "You're making quite an impact around here, young lady. Folks in Harmony Crick are going to remember you for a long time. Maybe you'll even decide to stay on a spell."

"I . . . well," Gwyn murmured. "I have obligations back in Chicago." At first she'd cared only if Neal remembered her, but now, strangely, Mae's words touched her heart and she wanted to reach out to others. Tonight's meeting would give her a chance to leave her signature as solid evidence of her support of what they needed.

AT THE LAST MINUTE that night Neal had an emergency call and had to wait for a patient. So Gwyn went to the meeting at the McPhersons' alone. She was learning to live with the constant disruptions to his well-laid plans.

More than twenty people crowded into the living room. The group was noisy, with everyone talking at once, ideas flowing, opinions flying. But when Mae stood up and bellowed for everyone to get quiet and listen, they did. She explained the petitions and handed them out to anyone who wanted to take them and get signatures. There would be an area rally in Ducktown next Saturday night and more petitions would be available then.

When the meeting was over, Gwyn was surprised to see W. T. Hancock, the twins' father. She shook his hand. "Nice to see you again, W.T. How did you get here? Isn't the creek still too high to drive through?"

"Yep. That's exactly why I'm here. Mighty inconvenient for families. Dangerous, too."

"That's why we're all here," she said fervently. "How's Debra? And the twins?"

"They're just fine. But I worry about how I'd get them across if they had an emergency right now." He shook his head in dismay. "Only that swinging bridge."

"And that thing's not fit for anyone. Your problem is exactly why we're all here signing petitions and fighting for that bridge." She smiled softly. "W.T., I'm honored that you named one of the girls after me. I can't tell you how much that means to me."

"Well, we figure you're a special lady. And pretty, too." His cheeks colored as he embarrassed himself complimenting her. "I'm supposed to invite you to dinner sometime, as soon as the creek goes down. Debra says she didn't get a chance to meet you properly."

"Why, thank you. I'd love to come to dinner sometime and have a chance to visit with Debra. We were all pretty busy that night, weren't we? I'm looking forward to holding my namesake again."

"Those babies are mighty fine." W.T. beamed with pride. "We'll be in touch. Bye now. And thanks for everything."

Gwyn turned away, feeling about as warm and wonderful as a person could. She was getting a taste of how Neal felt when he helped people in need and they came back later, forever grateful. It was a very good feeling, too.

Before she left, Gwyn was approached by a young woman with wispy blond hair. "Hello, I'm Sara Frazier. I understand the doctor is looking for a nurse."

"Yes." Gwyn studied the sincere young woman whom she'd never met.

"I'm a nurse. I live in the area. And I'm looking for a job."

Gwyn smiled. "Well, the doctor isn't here tonight, but if you'll come to the office, I'll be glad to set up an interview."

"You will? Oh, this is great."

"Do you live on the mountain?"

"No, but my parents do. And my mother has a heart ailment. She could need emergency care at any time and really needs the bridge. My husband and I plan to move up there, too, as soon as the bridge is completed. Right now, though, we can't be stranded on the other side of the creek when it floods. I have to be able to get to work."

"Where do you work now?"

Sara fidgeted with her purse. "I'm waiting tables in Murphy because I can't find work in my field."

Gwyn smiled reassuringly. "You may be just the one the doctor is looking for, Sara. Why don't you come by the office in the morning around ten and bring your credentials?"

"I have to work tomorrow. Could I come Wednesday?"

"Sure."

"And, uh, would you mind if I brought my husband? He's a computer whiz. At least to me, he seems like a whiz. I hear you're looking for office staff, too."

"Word gets around, doesn't it?"

"Representative Sanders called my nursing school in Chattanooga. And they called me. It sounded pretty important."

Gwyn was delighted with the response from the politician. She was glad to see he was working for the people of Harmony Creek. "Sure, your husband can come along."

"We just want to meet Dr. Perry. We've heard so much about him." She pumped Gwyn's hand. "Thank you!"

Gwyn could hardly wait to get home to tell Neal the good news. Apparently her pushy attitude with the media and the politician had produced the desired action. She almost forgot to bring along the stew and corn bread Mae had sent for Neal.

THE NEXT MORNING the telephone rang during breakfast. Neal answered, then pointed to Gwyn. She frowned. Travis? At this hour?

Her expression was thoroughly readable, and Neal covered the receiver. "It isn't him. Your boss, I think."

She wrinkled her nose and took the phone.

Ed's voice was loud and harsh. "Gwyn, what the hell is going on down there?"

"Nothing. Everything's fine. I've been busy with systems for ordering drugs and—"

"Gwyn, what's this I see on TV?"

"I...I don't know, Ed. What are you talking about?"

"Well, I was calmly watching the *Today* show, drinking my morning coffee, when I nearly choked! There, in living color, was my own Gwyn Frederick, telling how the SHARE program doesn't evaluate their systems well enough. And how there are so many other needs for this clinic where you're working. And why doesn't the state do more?"

"On national TV? Great!" She smiled at Neal, then the smile faded as Ed exploded.

"Not great! You're there to organize, not evaluate. I want you to keep a low profile. Stay out of local politics."

"That isn't politics, Ed. It's facts."

"The hell it isn't! I don't want Mark Time mentioned in the same article that describes state and federal waste."

"Oh, no..."

"You lay low until Friday. Then you hightail it home, you hear me?"

"Yes, sir." She hung up, now knowing whether to laugh or cry.

"Representative Sanders made it to the *Today* show, along with the 'bridge to nowhere' issue. And so did I."

"Ed's not happy, though."

She shook her head. "Not happy at all. Lay low, he says."

"Then you'd better do just that."

She looked at him and a determination grew inside her. "It's too late. I've already signed the petition."

"Well, we can get your name off."

She grabbed his arm. "Don't you dare. I signed that petition for little Elizabeth Gwyn. And I want my name to stay."

"Your boss will have a fit."

"I don't care."

"You're something special, Gwyn." He wrapped her in his arms.

"We're in this together, Neal," she said with conviction. "I'm going to do everything I can to help build that bridge."

"At the risk of your job?"

"It's no great risk." She looked at him defiantly. "Not compared to helping Elizabeth Gwyn."

9

In spite of Neal's protests to the contrary, they developed a routine, a flexible but steady schedule designed to accommodate as much as possible in their busy days. Gwyn worked diligently on the office systems and helped keep the flow of patients steady. There were, of course, unplanned emergencies. However, Gwyn was pleased with the few patients who called for routine appointments.

Gwyn developed systems for filing and supplies, then tackled billing. All systems were ready to be placed on a computer when funds became available. To her surprise and delight, the stream of pies and cakes was replaced almost entirely by salads and casseroles. She even worked out a barter system exchanging office cleaning for a certain amount of health care credit.

Most of the time Neal was able to take his forty-five-minute lunch break. He started receiving a local newspaper, claiming it was so he could follow his old favorite pro football team, the Miami Dolphins. But Gwyn knew it was also an opportunity for him to keep up with the general news, an indication that he was terminating his hermit days.

Ah, but their nights were made for loving. They would curl up in front of the fireplace, nibbling popcorn or merely watching the flames. When they could stay apart no longer, they'd make wild, passionate love.

Or they would go to bed and talk for hours, just holding each other close, in complete contentment.

What wasn't discussed was the dreaded knowledge that she would be leaving Saturday, in less than a week. The realization loomed too painfully, the solution too impossible.

On Wednesday Gwyn expected Sara and her husband. However, the prospective nurse, who had seemed so eager Monday night at Mae's to interview for the job, was late. Maybe she'd changed her mind. Oh, well, it had seemed too good to be true to find a nurse willing to locate in the remote area.

Gwyn glanced out the window again. It was a typical December morning in the Smokies. Sycamore and oak branches presented bare arms reaching toward gray skies. Evergreens dotted the countryside with nature's Christmas trees. This time of year, though, ominous weather was more likely to produce rain than snow.

At the clinic there were no signs of the impending Christmas season. Back in Chicago, red and green decorations and jingling bells had been in place since early November. It was a happy, festive time in the city, and Gwyn missed the gaiety, as well as the boisterous family gatherings. She had resolved to do something about it just as a pickup truck, driven by the blond nurse, pulled into the parking lot.

Gwyn stepped to the lab, where Neal was doing blood tests and setting up a couple of throat cultures. "She's here, Neal. And she brought her husband."

"I'll be right there." He finished making notes on the appropriate files, recalling the haphazard way he'd done this before Gwyn arrived. Now she made sure he had the correct file and pertinent information at his fingertips. Since she'd been here, influencing and organizing, he'd been able to see more patients in less time. And, of course, she didn't even attempt the nursing duties. With a nurse he could be doubly efficient, so he was anxious for this to work out.

He could hear Gwyn talking to a man and woman before he stepped into the waiting room. But he was surprised when he saw the young nurse's husband was in a wheelchair.

"Hi. I'm Dr. Perry." He strode forward and extended his hand to the woman. "Nice to meet you, Sara."

She smiled somewhat nervously. "Dr. Perry, this is my husband, Derrick Frazier." The two men shook hands, and she apologized to Gwyn for being late. "A traffic jam, would you believe? Actually they're working on the road from Ducktown. We were stopped for almost half an hour while they resurfaced a section of the blacktop. And just as we got started again, two cars had a minor accident that blocked both lanes for another half hour."

"Resurfacing?" Gwyn smiled happily. "Great!"

Sara looked puzzled. "I was afraid you'd be angry that we're late."

"Actually I'm more delighted that they're fixing the road."

"You see, Gwyn pushed Representative Sanders for a better road. Looks like she got it, too," Neal explained with a broad smile of congratulations directed at Gwyn. "She's the one responsible for getting the roads and a lot of other things around here fixed."

"Once again, proof that it pays to be the squeaky wheel," Gwyn said modestly. She was pleased, though, to get action on the road so quickly. She'd mention that in her report, too. Maybe when Ed totaled her accomplishments, he'd cool down over the fact that she'd gotten involved in the bridge business.

Neal leaned his hips on the desk and chatted amiably with the Fraziers. "Yes, this lady knows how to get things done. During the past week she's organized this office until it purrs with efficiency. From the beginning she's been talking about computerizing the paperwork and even has me halfway convinced it'll work."

"She's absolutely right," Derrick said with conviction. "An office with no computer system is functioning in the Dark Ages."

"We know where we stand, then," Neal said with a chuckle. "Trouble is, we have no money for such a system. And no one to run it."

Derrick scrutinized the shelves full of files. "It would take some time to feed those files into a system initially, but after that a part-time staffer could keep your records up-to-date."

"Could you do it?"

"Yes, I think so." Derrick met Neal's gaze directly.

Sara stepped forward and put her hand on Derrick's arm. "Last year Derrick's knees were crushed in a freak accident on the job. After recuperation the company sent him to school to learn a new trade in computers. He'll be finishing his course in January. So far, he's at the top of his class," she added proudly.

"Tell you what," Neal offered. "When you've completed the course, come back and see me about this. Meantime, I'll scout around and see if I can round up some federal money for a computer system."

Derrick smiled broadly. "It's a deal! Thank you, sir."

Gwyn made herself busy at the desk, allowing Neal to conduct the interview. After all, he'd be the one working with these people. Fortunately the waiting room was empty, so they had a few minutes of privacy.

Neal turned to Sara. "Tell me a little about yourself and why you want this job."

"I'm trained to be a nurse, but the only job I could get around here was as a waitress in Murphy. I want to utilize my training, and to be honest, we need for me to have a better paying job."

"Why didn't you stay in Chattanooga where you trained? I'm sure you could get a better paying job in a large hospital."

Sara looked tired. "While Derrick was still in therapy, my mother's heart condition was diagnosed. It was a time for family members to pull together, to help one another, and we decided to move back home. The only job I could find was in Murphy."

"Your parents live on Buck Mountain?"

"We'd like to move up there, too, as soon as they replace that darn bridge," she said. "Until then we're renting a small place near Ducktown. I have to be sure I can get to work. Right now, for instance, with the creek flooded, I wouldn't be able to get out."

"Any trauma care experience? We seem to have our share of emergencies here."

"Not much, but I'm unflappable in a crisis."

"I'll vouch for that," Derrick said. "She's as steady as a rock."

"Good." Neal showed them around the office, gave Sara a brief overview of what he expected and needed in a nurse and offered her the job. Plans were set for her to start on Friday so Gwyn could show her the business systems.

When the couple left, Gwyn put the Out to Lunch sign on the office door and followed Neal into his living quarters.

"What do you think?" he asked, pouring them each a glass of cider.

"Well, it's unfortunate that she has so little hands-on experience. On the plus side, you can train her to suit your needs and those of Harmony Creek. I think you had no other choice but to offer her the job." Gwyn opened a can of tomato soup and dumped it into a pot. "I believe she'll do fine. If she's, as Derrick says, steady in a crisis, she'll be a great asset to your office. I'm sure it's been a tough year for her."

"And Derrick?"

"I think he came along for several reasons," she said, pondering the situation as she sipped her cider. "He seemed to know what he was talking about. He's smart and capable and still very much a part of the family. I think he saw this as a possible job opportunity, too good to pass up." She shrugged. "He's right. Once the initial systems are in a computer, a part-time staffer could probably handle it. He may be able to work here, as well as other businesses in the area."

Neal hooked his arm around her waist from behind and pulled her close. "You know something, Gwyn? The impact you've made on my life in less than two weeks is remarkable."

"Representative Sanders is the man with the power to create change."

"But you were smart enough to capitalize on that fact." He turned her around and kissed her nose. "Everything's changing for the best."

She smiled tightly. "All but us."

"I have a suggestion."

"Yes?"

"Just stay."

Her mouth dropped open. "Stay here? And do what?"

"We'll make mad, passionate love every night."

"Nice. Very nice. But that's not a job."

"I'll pay full wages," he teased, and kissed her quickly.

"Why don't you come back to Chicago with me?" she posed. "It's great this time of year. I'll introduce you to my family, and you can have Christmas with us."

He shook his head before she even finished.

"Why not? You'll have a great time—"

He pushed away from her. "I'm not much for celebrating Christmas."

"So I see. But you'll love it with us." She reached for his hand. "And when the festivities are over, you can easily find a job in Chicago."

"No, Gwyn." He turned away from her.

"Why?"

"It . . . just wouldn't work out. I have patients. Martha Spears's baby is due. And—" he shrugged "—it just wouldn't work out."

"But I don't understand."

His jaw tightened; his lips became a tight line. "No, you don't. So drop it. I'm not going anywhere for the holidays." He stalked to his bedroom, leaving Gwyn to stare at the door. And wonder what in the world was wrong with him.

THOUGH IT REMAINED CLOUDY all day, it didn't rain. Late in the afternoon someone stopped by the office to announce the creek had gone down enough to drive through, and Neal decided to close the office early and go get his Jeep.

"I'll go with you," Gwyn volunteered, trying to mend the rift between them and add some cheerfulness to the air.

"And cross the bridge?"

She reconsidered. "I'll go as far as the bridge."

"Suit yourself." He pulled on his coat.

They walked in silence for a while until Gwyn could stand it no longer. "I'm sorry, Neal. It was selfish of me to suggest that you be the one to leave."

"I wonder if you really understand my commitment here, Gwyn."

"Does your commitment mean you can never leave? No days off? No vacation?"

"No. But now is not the time. Maybe next summer."

"And until then you'll be a workaholic?"

"If that's what you want to call me."

"I want . . . I want to be with you, Neal." She slipped her hand into his.

"And I want the same thing, Gwyn."

"But it has to be here, on your turf? Doesn't seem quite fair. You're a good doctor, Neal. You could work anywhere."

"I have a commitment here in Harmony Creek for another year and a half."

"Then what? Where will you go? Or will you stay here indefinitely?"

"Maybe. I don't know."

They reached the bridge, and Gwyn hung back, not wanting to get close to the thing. Neal reached for her and hugged her tightly. "I'll be a little while. I think I'll go see how Debra and the twins are doing."

"Give them my best."

"No, I'd rather save that for me."

She smiled at his attempt to lighten the mood. "Oh, Neal, I hate it when we're like this."

"So do I. And I hate thinking of you leaving, Gwyn. I don't know how I'm going to make it without you."

"Neal, that's ridiculous! You're very capable. You take care of everybody within a hundred miles. And you were making it fine before I came."

"No, not very well." He kissed her hungrily, his lips claiming hers in a warm affirmation of affection. "I'm missing you already. I've got to hurry so I can get back to your arms as quickly as possible. Se you in a couple of hours." He waved as he trotted onto the bridge.

Gwyn turned away quickly. The mere thought of him walking across that high, precarious swinging bridge sent cold chills down her spine. Even though she knew people crossed it daily, she feared it.

On her way home Gwyn was thrilled to notice her much-desired Christmas decorations growing naturally. In Chicago she had to pay dearly for twigs of evergreen, but here they were available for the taking. She found holly bushes, as well. But the greatest thrill was sighting bunches of mistletoe growing in the bare branches. Happily she gathered as much as she could carry. What a surprise she'd have for Neal when he returned.

IT WAS DARK when he drove up. From the outside the place looked especially cheerful and warm. He could see the fire blazing and hurried to get inside the warm little love nest he and Gwyn had created in the crude, barracks-type building. He thought of her waiting arms, her smile, her kiss, and he grew tight inside remembering her feminine delights. He'd been selfish and unfair earlier today. She couldn't be expected to understand his feelings about staying in Harmony Creek at this particular time. He was just now beginning to understand them himself. He vowed to make it up to her some way.

Neal bounded onto the porch and swung open the door. He froze, cringing from the impact to his senses. He was bombarded with Christmas.

Merry, bell-tinkling tunes. Arrangements of evergreen branches emitting the fragrance of pine. Circles of holly. Flickering candles. Pine boughs on the mantel. A warm fire. And before he could utter a word, Gwyn murmured something about mistletoe and began kissing him soundly.

When she finally paused for breath, he raised his head and mumbled gruffly, "What's all this?"

"Christmas has finally come to Harmony Creek!" She tugged off his coat and hung it on the coat rack, while he walked around the room, stunned.

"It's amazing."

"I knew you'd love it!" She took his hand and led him to the fireplace so he could admire the special arrangement she'd made on the mantel. "Do you know that I'd have to pay dearly in Chicago for all this? When we were younger, my dad would take us all out into the country to search for pine boughs. But in recent years we just bought wreaths in the city, already made. And holly is a special treat. Sometimes we'd use the fake stuff because we couldn't find anything reasonable." She reached out and touched a couple of items. "Aren't these pine cones great? But the greatest is the mistletoe! Growing free for the taking."

His eyes were glazed. "I wish you hadn't gone to the trouble, Gwyn."

"It wasn't much trouble. I enjoyed doing it. We've been too busy for the spirit of Christmas around here, and I've missed it. Don't you like it?" There was a moment of uncomfortable silence, then she gasped. "Oh, no! You aren't allergic to all this pine, are you?"

"No."

"Then what's wrong with it? Oh, dear! Does the forest belong to someone who doesn't want the trees trimmed?"

He shook his head and looked around. He wanted to escape, but she'd stuck a branch or pine cone all around the room. There was no place to get away from them.

"I didn't mean any harm, Neal. I just missed all the holiday festivities. I thought you'd like a few reminders of Christmas. That's all."

"A few? This place is overrun with them! I don't need any reminders of Christmas."

"Why not?"

He ran his hand through his hair and took a ragged breath. "It's . . . it's just not for me."

She stared at him. From the looks of him she'd done something terribly wrong, but she had no idea what. "Why, Neal?" she asked softly, not knowing what else to ask. She had to get him to explain.

He turned away from her, his blurred gaze focusing on a candle's flickering flame. "It's a difficult time, okay? Please, just don't bother." He stalked into his bedroom and closed the door.

Gwyn stood there, stunned, listening to the strains of "Hark, the Herald Angels Sing." Refusing to accept his weak explanation, she knocked lightly on his door and entered. He was stretched out on the bed, hands folded beneath his head. He gazed blankly at the ceiling.

"Neal, I'd like to know what's really wrong with you."

He didn't answer.

She walked in and sat on the edge of the bed by his feet. She touched them, wrapping her hands around them as she talked. "I've been trying all day to please you, to let you know how much I care about you. And I've gone wrong at every turn. The funny thing is, I don't know what I've done wrong."

"It isn't you, Gwyn." His tone softened, but he still didn't look at her. "It's nothing."

"Nothing? That was quite a reaction in there, Neal, Apparently I triggered something pretty strong."

"As I said, it isn't you. It's me. So please, just forget it."

"I can't do that, Neal."

He turned his head toward the opposite wall. "Leave me alone."

"No. I care too much. Tell me what's troubling you. I deserve to know."

"Deserve?" He scoffed. "It has nothing to do with you, Gwyn."

"It does when I have to walk on eggshells to keep from offending you. This kind of behavior isn't like you."

"Humph."

"I know the man I've been with for almost two weeks is not the one who stalked out of the room a few minutes ago."

"Okay!" He turned back to her, his eyes intense and hard. "Okay, it's the memories that come along with the season."

Gwyn shifted and looked down. "The reminders of her?"

"Yes."

"The reminders that make you feel guilty you're enjoying something and she isn't? That you're alive and Maria isn't?"

He was silent, but she could hear his labored breathing.

"Yes," he said finally, his voice rough and hoarse.

"She must have died this time of year."

"Yes. And all this just reminds me of her. Too much." He sighed. "Gwyn, I'm sorry. I didn't want the past to interfere with us. Or for you to think—Oh, hell, I don't know."

"I think I know what you're trying to say." She placed her hand on his leg. "You loved her. It's all right, Neal. And I understand why you're so upset to be bombarded with reminders."

They were quiet for a few moments. Gwyn could hear a cheery Christmas carol in the background and the friendly crackle of the fire in the fireplace. The blaze had been started with love in her heart, the love she felt now for Neal. She knew he was hurting but wasn't sure what to do about it. There had to be something. She was a great believer in talking, in getting troubles out in the open. "Tell me about her, Neal. What happened to her?"

"You don't want to know."

"Yes, I do," Gwyn said softly, moving to his side, tucking one hand around his knee. "It was Christmastime. Was she ill?"

"No." He began hesitantly. "She was a nurse. Worked with me in the emergency room." Before he realized it, Neal was telling Gwyn the story he'd held inside himself too long. "We worked the midnight shift together. A . . . crazed man came in . . . very late. He stood in the hall shouting 'Merry Christmas to all!' We all thought he was just a poor drunk, until he began to spray bullets in a circle. For God's sake, he was carrying a gun and no one had noticed. It was so . . . so damned fast. Then he turned the gun on himself. They found out later he was high on drugs. But that didn't help."

"People were hurt?"

"Maria happened to be in the line of fire. She . . . she was hit. And died in my arms."

"I'm sorry." Gwyn's arms went around Neal in the darkness, and she held him close. "Oh, God, Neal, I'm so sorry."

"I could do nothing for her. I tried everything—we all did. But it was useless. We were absolutely helpless. The worst thing in the world for a doctor is not to be able to save the most important people to him, the ones he loves."

Gwyn pressed his head to her breast and cried silent tears for Neal. They lay like that for a long, long time. Finally she moved.

"Don't go," he murmured.

"I'll be back. I have something to do." She slipped from the bed and into the living room. Hurriedly she began to gather her decorations, scooping them into a bag.

"Gwyn. Gwyn, stop." Neal was beside her, gripping her arm. "Leave them. It's okay."

"I don't mind, Neal, now that I know why. I understand. I don't want to torment you with reminders of her. And of what happened."

He took the bag from her and began to distribute the greenery again. "I want it here. It's perfectly natural to have signs of Christmas, the way life should be this time of year. I've been a hermit too long." He turned back to her and took her in his arms. "Anyway, these now remind me of you. And of all the beauty we've shared."

"Oh, Neal . . ." She was lost in his kiss and his warm embrace.

He swept her up in his arms. "I think it's time we celebrated the season." And he carried her into the bedroom.

She kissed his neck. "I want to give you some good memories of the season."

And as they came together that night, Gwyn knew she loved him. Loved him more than she should. She had given her heart and lost her soul to a man who couldn't love her, not because he didn't want to but because someone else held his heart. And there would be nothing in this relationship for her except heartache. But she couldn't help herself. She loved him.

Through the night she showed him ways she loved him with her body. But she carefully hid the sadness she felt. Only after he slept, sated and content in her arms, did she release her sadness. And tears fell on the dark hair of the man who slept with his head against her breast.

10

NEAL'S STARTLING REVELATION made a difference in Gwyn's attitude, if not her actions. Sadly, she'd fallen in love with a man who couldn't love her. He was caught up in his past. She tried to convince herself that the best thing for her to do would be to go back to Chicago and try to forget their brief affair. She felt that in time Neal would also forget. The hardest part for her would be to forget the wonderful man she had loved so quickly.

For her last night in Harmony Creek, they had accepted an invitation for dinner with the Hancock family.

"Are you sure you wouldn't prefer to do something more, uh, special on your last night here?" He wanted her all to himself.

"This is special to me. Honest." She welcomed the idea of being around others on this most difficult evening. Otherwise she might crumble. And she had to remain strong.

"Buck Mountain isn't exactly an exciting place," he grumbled.

"Where would you suggest? Should we kick up our heels in Ducktown?" She checked her watch and snapped her fingers. "Oops, they've rolled up the sidewalks by now. We just missed the big event. Or maybe you'd prefer the bright lights and big city of Murphy."

He nodded, and his eyes brightened. "We could drive up to Eagle Ridge."

"Later," she promised with a smile. "Actually I'm looking forward to seeing the Hancocks. You forget I come from a growing family. I'm used to evenings like this. Anyway, the twins are a week old, and I can't wait to see them. Wonder how much they've grown." She checked her purse. "Uh-oh. Forgot my camera. I'll be right back."

She darted to her room, which she'd used only for changing her clothes during the past week. When she returned, she couldn't resist capturing a shot of Neal as he waited for her, leaning against the doorframe, hands stuffed in his pockets. It was a view of him she would preserve in her heart forever. "Hold it. I want to see if the battery works."

He didn't move when the light flashed, just stood there, watching her.

"You didn't mind, did you?" She pushed the camera into her purse and took his hand. "I want to take back snapshots of our namesakes."

He looked at her curiously. "What'll you tell the folks back home about the fellow in that picture?"

"I'll tell them what a fantastic doctor you are. And what a wonderful man." Her voice dwindled, and she took a deep breath. "I probably won't show this one around. It'll be in my private collection."

He lifted her hand and pressed it to his lips. "Ah, Gwyn, I wish it didn't have to be this way."

"Me, too," she whispered, near tears. But she had to remain strong, had to pretend she wasn't falling apart inside.

"I'm not great with goodbyes."

"Neither am I. That's why we need to spend this evening with friends." She stood on tiptoe and kissed his cheek. "Now since we can't call and say we've been detained, let's head up the mountain before it rains or does something equally drastic to prevent our travel."

Or to prevent your leaving, Neal thought miserably. He followed Gwyn out the door, wondering why he'd allowed himself to get involved with a woman he knew wouldn't hang around. Maybe that was why. She was safe. He had known from the beginning that she would leave. And he could go back to being a workaholic hermit, taking care of the folks of Harmony Creek.

He would be foolish to kid himself, though. Things were different since Gwyn had entered his life. *He* was different, too. She was a dynamo who made an impression on everyone she touched and had the remarkable ability to rectify whatever she considered wrong. Or make a valiant attempt. He would be reminded of her by everything from the gravel in the parking lot to checkups for the Hancock twins. Even the food he ate and his lunch schedule had been affected by Gwyn.

He wouldn't be able to inoculate little Elizabeth Gwyn without remembering the dark-haired woman responsible for her name. The one he'd made love to. He wouldn't be able to provide a routine checkup for little Amanda Nell without recalling the woman who had bravely stood by his side as he'd delivered those babies. And her tear-filled, chocolate-colored eyes when he'd told her their names.

But all those things were tangible. More elusive to detect and more difficult to pinpoint were what was going on inside him. Would his thoughts, his feelings and emotions ever be the same? He knew instinctively that she had changed him, too.

Their arrival at the Hancocks' was a festive event. Grandma Amanda had come from North Carolina to help with the twins and the household chores during the holidays. Whatever made Neal think this would be a dull, boring evening on Buck Mountain?

The minute the door opened, they were bombarded with Christmas, from the decorated tree in the corner to savory fragrances of a table laden with enough food for an army to the noisy, excited children.

The three young ones who'd been sleeping the night the twins were born surrounded Gwyn as she passed out little bags of goodies she'd purchased at the general store in Ducktown. Debra was delighted with her gifts of drawstring baby gowns for the twins. W.T. proudly showed off the smokehouse where he'd smoked the ham they ate for dinner. Even young Billy Joe displayed some of his wood carvings.

The best part of the evening for Neal was watching Gwyn's reactions while she took snapshots of the whole family as well as the infants. It was apparent she was enjoying the visit with the Hancock family. By the time they left the mountain, Neal realized that part of her reaction was because she missed her own family. And he understood a little of why she had to return to Chicago. Or he told himself he did.

Their lovemaking that night was especially heated. In the warm, flickering light of a candle left burning on the dresser, they stripped. Their nude bodies took on a burnished glow as they came together one last time.

She stroked his bearded face with gentle fingers, roving over every angle and plane. Framing his face, she kissed him, teasing the edges of his lips with her tongue.

"I want to remember you just like this. Your face, your nose, your lips, even your beard," she whispered.

"I want..." he began, then halted and continued. "I want you to come back, Gwyn. Someday. Please promise me you will."

A sob caught in her throat, and she wished she weren't leaving. They both knew she had to leave now. Returning, though, was another thing. In the dark of his room, as they held each other, Gwyn couldn't deny his wish. "I will," she promised in a whisper.

He responded by kissing her passionately. The kiss lengthened, he held her tightly as his body grew taut and warm next to hers.

"Neal," she murmured when they finally came up for air, "I want you to know how very special these two weeks in Harmony Creek have been to me. I didn't want to come at first. Now I think it's been the most enlightening—no, rewarding experience of my life."

"That's quite a testimony."

"And so has knowing you." She stroked his chest, then trailed her hand sensuously over the firm muscles lacing his stomach, and lower.

With a groan he caressed her shoulders and back. "Ah, Gwyn. You've given me so much...so much of yourself. You've made my life interesting again." He laid her back on the pillow, placing her arms above her head. With small, sensuous kisses he moved down the sensitive inner skin of both arms.

She shivered with delight and felt her nipples grow tight. She arched toward him, and he moved over her.

Rooting his wide-spread fingers in her hair, he kissed her again, moving from her lips to her temples and forehead. "I love your hair," he murmured as he kissed her cheeks and nose and eyelids. "Love your face, love your body. . ." He moved to her breasts, letting his lips play along and kiss the hard nipples.

When his tongue laved them, she arched and moaned for more. Gwyn responded eagerly to his touch, wanting his body, wanting to please. And letting him know it.

Neal was gentle and appreciative, prolonging each treasured moment. But when desire pushed him to a certain point, he loved her hungrily, as if he couldn't get enough. They complemented each other in bed as they did in life, sharing and accommodating, teasing and taunting, until they brought out the best and hottest in each other.

Sprinkling moist kisses over her silky skin, he soon drew her to the brink of ecstasy. When she urged his fulfillment with eager hands, he drove into her with a vigor that soon sent him over the edge.

Gwyn's climb was slower, more intense, as she relinquished herself to the mixed feelings of sharing her body with a man she would never forget, could never stop loving. And knowing that, in the process, she lost her heart. She moved with him, feeling his tension being released into her, and she whirled into the vortex of a high-level, emotional climax. When he slumped, relaxed, over her, tears of hopelessness mingled with those of joy to roll down her cheeks.

His kisses said *I love you*. His eyes, his hands, his body all said it. But not his voice. With a resigned sigh of acceptance she understood that he couldn't.

They slept fitfully, rolling apart, turning together, once waking enough to make love again, as if neither could bear parting. And yet they must.

MORNING BROUGHT a cold drizzle. The whole world, it seemed, was crying.

They didn't talk much. There wasn't much to say. Sara had agreed to come over to watch the office while Neal took Gwyn to Chattanooga to catch her plane. It would shorten the journey and give her a few more private hours with him.

Dressed for the trip, they were drinking a second cup of coffee, when they heard a truck out front. Gwyn's Gucci bags were stacked by the door, waiting for the journey back to Chicago.

"Sara's early, isn't she?" Neal commented sourly, his tone revealing resentment of an interruption to these last few minutes he and Gwyn had to share at Harmony Creek.

Gwyn raised her head to listen. "Sounds like a truck." She went to the window and peered through the heavy, gray mist. But it wasn't Sara's truck. A strained voice shouted, and she could see a man running through the rain. "Neal, it's Clyde Nelson. Something's wrong."

Before the words were completely out of her mouth, Neal was on his feet, responding to the pounding at the door. Gwyn moved right behind him.

Clyde Nelson loomed on the front porch, soaked to the skin and ashen faced. "Kane's been shot! The boys were quail hunting—"

"How bad?"

"His leg . . . bleeding a lot!"

"Let's get him into the clinic." Neal turned to Gwyn and barked orders as he started out into the drizzle with Clyde. "Unlock the office door. Get a room ready. Call Sara!"

Gwyn was breathing hard and her hands were shaking as she obeyed his instructions. She threw open the doors to the clinic and spread a clean sheet on the narrow examining room table, then went to the phone. She was dialing Sara's number when the men brought the Nelson youth into the office and carried him directly into the next room.

Clyde was right. The bleeding was profuse, making a crimson trail across the floor. A nervous teenager about the same age as Kane followed them inside. He wore a camouflage hunting suit and looked about as helpless and miserable as a person could.

The phone connection drew her attention. "Derrick, this is Gwyn at the clinic. We need Sara—it's an emergency."

"She's on her way. What's wrong?"

"A gunshot victim. Talk to you later." She hung up and glanced at the youth in the camouflage suit. He was obviously agitated. Her heart went out to him. "You were hunting with them?"

The boy's turmoil bubbled over, and he blurted out, "It was an accident. I didn't mean to do it."

She nodded. "I'm sure. Well, have a seat. This may take a while." She could hear Clyde talking to Neal in the adjoining room. It was a strange, one-sided conversation, because Neal wasn't responding. Clyde was just nervously babbling. She stepped to the examining-room door. "Neal, Sara's on her way. What can I do?"

Neal was frantically ripping open some packaged equipment. "Get sterilized towels from supplies. Lots of them. And the IV hook on the bottom shelf."

She hurried back, her arms loaded with his requests.

Neal was starting an IV in the boy's arm. He didn't even look up at her, just gave more instructions. "Get the scissors from the top drawer and cut his pants off, right up the leg. Take a couple of towels and press them to the wound until I get over there. We've gotta stop the bleeding. Fast."

She proceeded to do as Neal instructed. Suddenly her hands weren't shaking anymore. She just functioned like an automaton. It didn't even bother her when a spray of blood hit her blouse. She looked at the boy and was shocked to see his pain-filled eyes focused on her. He was awake during this whole experience. She figured he must be very scared. Gwyn swallowed hard. She was scared, too, but something urged her to reassure him.

She smiled weakly. "Kane, can you hear me?"

He blinked, and she took that as an affirmative.

"You're going to be okay. Dr. Perry's got everything under control. You're in good hands."

Vaguely, in the background, she could hear Clyde's nervous voice. He still hadn't hushed. Neal moved close to her, pulling on rubber gloves. He jerked his head toward Clyde and mumbled, "Get him outta here. He's driving me crazy. And call the helicopter emergency service in Chattanooga. I want Kane flown out as soon as possible."

She nodded as Neal took her place beside the injured boy. Grim-faced and concentrating on the wound, he began talking to Kane. His tone was surprisingly light. "How're you doing, buddy? You might feel a little dizzy now, but it'll be better soon. I'll give you something for the pain in a few minutes. You just hang in there. Talk to me. Can you tell me what happened?"

Gwyn took Clyde firmly by the arm. "Come on, Clyde. Let's give the doctor room to work." They entered the waiting room just as Sara opened the office door. "Thank goodness you're here! Neal needs you in there. Clyde's son has a gunshot wound."

"It was an accident," the teenager in the waiting room said to whoever would listen. "Uncle Clyde, I didn't mean to shoot him. Honestly, I couldn't help it. He just walked in my path."

"You two, sit," Gwyn instructed with a nod to the chairs that lined the wall. "And be quiet so I can call the emergency service."

Sara disappeared into the examining room, and Gwyn proceeded with her next duty. When the emergency helicopter was notified and on the way, she turned her attention to the nervous pair. "Waiting's always the worst, isn't it? How about something to drink? Orange juice or Coke?"

"Thank you, ma'am. A Coke sounds great." The teenager stood and rubbed his palms against his thighs. "I didn't mean to do it. I swear."

"We know you didn't. It was an accident," Gwyn said gently. She didn't know who was worse here: the guilty kid, the worried father or the injured Kane. But they all needed attention and care.

Clyde gave a low moan. "I . . . I need to call my wife and let her know Kane's been injured."

"Yes, you should. Come with me." Gwyn put her arm around his shoulders and led him into the living quarters to the phone. While he talked to the boy's mother, Gwyn poured an orange juice and opened a Coke. She whisked past her Gucci bags, still beside the door, the trip to Chicago forgotten.

Waiting was agony, even for Gwyn. The little room where Neal and Sara were treating the injured boy was very quiet. The minutes seemed to drag. At least, when she was in the heart of the action, she was busy and not thinking of what might happen if anything went wrong.

She tried chatting with the two who waited with her and discovered the teenager was Kane's cousin from Knoxville, who'd never been hunting. When he'd come to the mountains for a visit, the Nelsons took him quail hunting. Unfortunately the adventure had ended in disaster.

Eventually Neal emerged from the room, peeling off his rubber gloves.

Clyde stood anxiously. "How is he, Doc?"

"For now he's stabilized. The bleeding's curtailed until we can fly him to Chattanooga for surgery."

"Surgery? Is he going to be all right?"

"Yes, I think so."

When Mrs. Nelson arrived, panic evident in her face, Neal took her by the hand and led her into the examining room to see her son. Neal was gentle and calming in the face of these people's panic. Gwyn was thoroughly impressed.

In a little more than an hour the rescue helicopter arrived. They loaded the injured boy and airlifted him out, taking Clyde along. Mrs. Nelson took her nephew back home to make plans to go to the Chattanooga hospital. And suddenly, after chaos, everyone was gone and everything in the clinic was quiet.

Neal, Gwyn and Sara worked for a while, cleaning up the mess. Finally Sara hauled a bundle of soiled sheets to the door. She glanced around. "Is this all?"

Neal looked at her approvingly. "Well, for your first test, Sara, you did fine. Thanks. And you, Gwyn, were great. I realize a trauma like this can be quite unnerving, but you did okay. Because everybody pulled together calmly, the patient is going to live."

Sara smiled at Neal, obviously pleased. "You know, this was the first time in months that my work has been so rewarding. *This* is what I'm trained to do—nursing. I'm just glad I could be here to help. Thanks for the job, Dr. Perry." She glanced at Gwyn. "Is it too late for you to go to Chattanooga now?"

"What?" Gwyn looked stunned. She'd forgotten all about her flight back to Chicago. For the past two hours all she'd thought about was the emergency at hand. She glanced at her watch. "I couldn't possibly make it now."

"Oh, no." Sara shook her head. "When does the next flight leave?"

Gwyn sighed and looked at Neal. His clothes were a mess. Then she looked down at her own. They were terrible. "I don't think I'm going anywhere today."

"Well, if that's the case, I'll be heading back home," Sara said. "I'll drop these off at the laundry. See you on Monday."

Gwyn and Neal waved goodbye to Sara, then exchanged long looks. "Do you believe in fate?" he asked finally.

"I didn't until today. Do you think..." She halted and shook her head. "Naw."

He shrugged. "Whatever the reason, we're still here. You've missed your flight. You're stuck for another night."

"You—" she gestured "—you look awful, Doctor."

"So do you, Assistant. I think we need a shower.

"And to wash these clothes immediately in cold water before they're ruined." She hesitated. "But first I'd better make a phone call and tell someone in Chicago I won't be arriving today."

He nodded silently and followed her into the living quarters. "You know, Gwyn, you're terrific. I really appreciate the way you handled yourself in there. Most people couldn't have done what you did. Thanks for helping to save that boy's life."

She looked at him, aghast. "You don't have to thank me for helping out in such an emergency. I just did what I could. It wasn't much."

"It was to me. And to the Nelsons." He put his arm around her shoulders. "When pressed into duty, you always come through. For a city gal, you're really something."

She put her arms around his waist and looked up into his beautiful eyes, wanting in that moment to sink into their azure depths. "So are you, Neal. Do you realize what you did in there? With absolutely no hesitation, you took care of that kid. I know it must have been difficult, since it must have brought back such painful memories of what happened that night to Maria."

"You know, I didn't . . . even . . . think of . . . her." He gazed across the room at nothing in particular, a strange expression in his eyes. "You're right. I did it. There was a time when I thought I could never handle a trauma case, much less a gunshot victim. I even wanted to get out of trauma care altogether. That's why I picked Harmony Creek Clinic. I thought everything that came through here would be head colds, inoculations and delivering babies."

"I'm very proud of you, Neal."

"The only thing I could think of in there was saving Kane Nelson's life."

She pressed him to her with a long hug. "I'm glad we were still here to help."

"Even though we missed your plane?"

"If we hadn't been here, he might have died."

"Yes, it's likely." He sighed heavily. "Well, we'll try to make it tomorrow."

"Or the next day."

He pulled back. "Or...what?"

"Or maybe...even...next week." She grinned slowly, as a daring idea began to take shape. "Doesn't your new nurse need some extra training in the systems I've installed? Don't you need some extra office help?"

He laughed aloud and whirled her off her feet in a bear hug. "Don't I need you? Yes, yes, yes!"

LATER, WITH SOUNDS of the washing machine in the background sloshing their clothes, Gwyn sat down at the phone. She pulled her bathrobe tighter across her breasts, took a deep breath and dialed Travis's number. When he answered, she blurted out her reason for calling. "I'm glad I caught you, Travis. An emergency came up, and I missed the plane."

"You *what*?"

"We had an emergency at the clinic this morning and—"

Travis interrupted. "How could you do something so stupid as—"

"Please, Travis, it's been a difficult morning. It couldn't be helped."

"Why didn't you plan better? What could possibly have been more important than your coming home?"

"A teenager had a hunting accident and almost died," she said brutally, suddenly angry. "I consider that more important than anything."

"Well, I suppose," he mumbled. "When's the next flight?"

"I...uh, please tell Ed I'm taking another week. The doctor just hired a nurse, and I need to spend a little

more time training her in office management procedures."

"Another week? That's absolutely ridiculous!"

"It's what I'm going to do."

"Gwyn, what's going on there? You sound different."

"Maybe I am, Travis. I'll talk to you later. Pick me up
same time, next Saturday, please." She hung up and
looked at Neal with a little smile. Different? She certainly was . . . especially in her heart.

Neal, wearing only his briefs, took her hands and
pulled her to her feet. "Gwyn, are you sure?"

She pressed one palm to his warm, vibrant chest.
"I'm sure. It means I get to attend the rally for the 'bridge
to nowhere' tonight."

"You might be risking your job."

"I don't think I can risk it much more than I already
have. I'll keep a low profile. Anyway, this is important."

He kissed her fingertips. "It means we have another
week together."

"That's the most important thing to me," she said
with a warm smile. Her brown eyes softened as he bent
to kiss her.

"It sounds glorious to me," he mumbled between
kisses. "How about a shower? I'm good at scrubbing
backs."

"Yes, yes, yes!" She laughed as he picked her up and
carried her to the bedroom.

11

"I DON'T KNOW WHY I didn't think of this earlier!"

"Making love? We were too busy."

"Criteria of effective goals." She sighed and placed his palm against her cheek. "Change, amend and rearrange."

"Why, sure. I think of those things all the time. But not now." He nuzzled her earlobe and whispered, "Well, maybe rearrange."

"It fits."

"Of course we do."

"They're terms from my time management seminars," Gwyn explained. "And they fit my circumstances exactly. 'Be flexible enough to change your goals.' I've certainly done that here."

"You are not unyielding," he murmured, trailing kisses down her cheek to her chin, then down her chin to her neck.

"Neal . . ." She laughed as he continued to tempt her. "I've amended priorities with every unexpected event or crisis. And there've been plenty of those around here."

"My life revolves around chaos. And you've adjusted nicely." His kisses dipped lower, and the movement brushed each taut nipple with his mustache. "But some events follow a natural order. Like now . . ."

"And now it's time to rearrange."

"That's what I've been saying all along."

"Rearrange my schedule," she insisted with a little giggle. "So we can spend more time together."

"That, too," he muttered as he pulled her over his chest and quieted her with a mind-spinning kiss that seemed to last forever.

As she lay in his arms, Gwyn had no doubts that this was exactly where she belonged. Time choices, she'd been taught, were made on either rational or emotional levels. The rational was planned, organized and usually produced the best use of time. Gwyn decided she had functioned on that level far too long. Now was the time for a purely emotional choice. And she'd never been happier.

That night at the "bridge to nowhere" rally in Ducktown, Neal spoke to the crowd about the people on Buck Mountain and how they needed the bridge. He cited real events, most recently the home delivery of twins on the mountain and the potential for disaster in that instance. Gwyn, bursting with pride, joined the crowd's enthusiastic cheers as Neal left the podium. There were a series of speakers, mostly politicians who took advantage of the opportunity to reiterate their support.

Not surprisingly, the audience was dotted with news reporters. With good intentions Gwyn made a conscious effort to stay out of the line of photographers' cameras. But one reporter managed to squeeze a tiny conversation from her before she slipped away in the crowd with Neal.

On Sunday evening they heard that the young gunshot victim, Kane Nelson, was doing well after surgery. Kane's grandmother brought over a traditional Southern chess pie along with the good news. But the gratitude in her eyes was the best reward. Gwyn knew that when she flew back to Chicago the next weekend, she would take with her the memory of that grandmother's beautiful expression thanking them both for saving her grandson's life.

She would also carry a wealth of memorable days and nights of loving Neal. The extra week became a treasury of cherished moments for two people discovering love. Gwyn had never been loved like this before, and she was constantly preoccupied with the doctor.

For Neal, being with Gwyn was a precious new experience. For the first time in two years he was enjoying being intimate with a woman and learning to laugh and love again. And yet he couldn't hold her in Harmony Creek.

As GWYN'S PLANE FLEW out of Chattanooga the next Saturday, Neal watched Gwyn leave with a sad heart, knowing full well he might never see her again. Gwyn evaluated the time she'd spent at Harmony Creek. On a rational level it was one of the most productive efforts she had ever managed. She and Sara had honed the systems Gwyn had initially put into place, making sure the office hummed with efficiency along with sound medical care. Knowing she'd provided a much-needed service for others gave her a wealth of satisfaction. Perhaps it wasn't for glory, but the rewards were there, just the same.

On an emotional level, though, Gwyn was a wreck. She felt close to those whose lives she had touched directly and had a great deal of affection for them. Amazingly, during the week her love for Neal had grown. She hadn't thought it possible.

As the plane rose steadily above the cloud layers, taking her away from him, she was overwhelmed with emptiness and a distinct sadness. It was almost like leaving her family.

How would she function without him? She told herself life would continue just as it had before they'd met. But in her heart she knew better. She was different because of him. At this moment she understood a small portion of the pain he must have endured after his lover was killed.

And she loved him even more.

TRAVIS MET HER at O'Hare Airport. As they drove to her apartment, she felt no sense of gladness at being home. In truth, she was emotionally drained because of leaving Neal and Harmony Creek. It was strange, since she hadn't seen Harmony Creek until three weeks ago. Still, there was a distinct feeling of loss. She'd promised Neal she would return. But would she? What if he forgot her and their brief liaison? What if the feelings between them dwindled?

They entered her upstairs flat, and Travis placed her bags in the tiny foyer. "Glad to be home, Gwyn?"

"Mmm." She dropped her purse on a chair and ambled into the neatly arranged combination living-dining room.

"It's been so long since you've been to the office that I may have to introduce you around," he quipped, following her into the room. "I couldn't believe you opted to stay there an extra week. Something must have really grabbed your attention."

Attention? she mused. How about heart? She sighed and walked between the sofa and matching chair. "Two weeks just wasn't enough. My work wasn't finished.

There were still so many things to do, and I hated to leave it half done. We had just hired a nurse, who didn't know the doctor's procedures or my newly created systems. I needed a longer period to train her. Even with an extra week I left much to be done."

"You understand that the extra week was your own time, don't you?"

She nodded.

"Working with no salary?" He squinted at her. "That isn't like you, Gwyn. Needless to say, Ed is furious with you."

"I'm sure." She laughed nervously. "Well, he said this assignment wasn't for glory. And he was right."

"Don't you think your contribution to the little clinic was over and above the call of duty?"

"You wouldn't believe how great the needs are in Harmony Creek." She turned to him with wide eyes. "While I was there, I barely scratched the surface. I guess I got caught up in the problems."

"Is that why you were a part of that political hot potato?"

She raised her brows, recognizing the acid in his tone. "You mean the bridge?"

"Exactly! That was a ridiculous thing for you to become involved in, Gwyn. A 'bridge to nowhere' indeed! And everything you did just set Ed off again. I . . . couldn't explain your behavior."

She stiffened. "Why should you, Trav? You don't have to take responsibility for my behavior."

"As team leader, and the one staying in touch with you, I felt somewhat responsible. You know how Ed is."

"And another thing!" She faced him squarely with arms folded. "For your information, the proposed structure isn't a 'bridge to nowhere.' It will lead somewhere important. To people. The communities at Harmony Creek and Buck Mountain need that bridge. And they deserve it."

She took a deep breath and continued. "Somebody has to help them stand up to the opposition. And that's what Neal, er, the doctor and I did. The people can't help the floods that washed the old one away! Now the funds are available, but others want to use the money to satisfy their own selfish needs." She turned away and glared out the window.

"Do you realize how you sound right now, Gwyn? Give you a soapbox and you'd go to work on me." He gestured and followed her across the room. "Even after Ed told you to lay off, you attended some damned rally and got your opinions in the newspaper again."

"What? How did you know about that?"

"It was in the papers here! The whole situation is the laughing stock of the metropolitan area. City folks versus country folks. Big city editors know what sells papers. So they send a bunch of reporters to the little local skirmishes." He leaned forward from the waist, as if he were disciplining a child. "And you gave them just what they wanted! A story about those mountain people being as important as those who want to build condos in the city."

"Well, they are!"

He shook his head in dismay. "Didn't make a good impression on Ed, I'll tell you."

Gwyn turned away from his angry tirade. "I had no idea they'd quote me."

"Maybe it's because you're so damned quotable!"

"But important people made speeches. The state representative, for Pete's sake! He's a big cheese in that state."

"But they were quoting you! They were probably delighted to find some bleeding heart Yankee who had flown into Appalachia from the big city of Chicago to organize their floundering little clinic and gotten wrapped up in some nonsensical local cause."

"It isn't nonsense! That's what I've been trying to tell you. It's vital!" She turned on him, her brown eyes flashing. "The clinic isn't floundering, either! They have a fine physician who was taking care of everyone and everything before I arrived and is certainly capable of doing the same now that I'm gone. I just organized a few things. And furthermore, I'm no bleeding heart! But anybody with any sensitivity for people would want to help them!"

"Listen to yourself, Gwyn, and tell me you aren't a little bit bizarre."

"If I raved on about their inadequate schedules and systems, you'd probably be near tears, Travis. But when I talk about real people who are having babies and surviving heart attacks and recovering from gunshot wounds because of one excellent physician, you stiffen up and close me out. Is it because you don't care about real people?"

"Of course I do. But I can keep a perspective."

"Harmony Creek has affected my life."

He nodded slowly. "It certainly has. And what else? The bridge? The people? Also, the doctor?"

She turned away and buried her face in her hands. The situation was falling apart rapidly. She was losing her cool and her perspective. If she didn't get control of herself, the next day at work would be an even worse disaster. "I'm tired now, Travis. Let's discuss this later."

"Sure." He headed for the door. "Glad to have you back, Gwyn. See you at work tomorrow."

"See ya. Thanks for picking me up at the airport."

He shrugged. "All in a day's work. Get some rest, Gwyn, so you can hit it with both feet running tomorrow."

Gwyn walked him to the door, then locked it securely after him. She roamed her apartment in the growing darkness, trying to revive her spirits. She was home. She should be glad.

But she wasn't.

Finally she went back to the living-room window. In daylight the view of her street wasn't spectacular, but at night the lights made the place appear beautiful, almost glamorous. At this time of year it looked especially festive with Christmas decorations and multicolored lights. More people than usual bustled along the street, carrying packages, all appearing happy. But Gwyn had never felt more unhappy. And alone.

What she needed was . . . Neal.

Maybe her family would help. She thought about calling her mother to tell her she was back. But for some reason she didn't want to make contact with her old familiar turf just yet. She wanted to relish her Harmony Creek experiences and try to weigh them against Chicago.

There was no comparison. They were two different worlds.

Her thoughts wandered to Neal. What was he doing right now? Had he eaten the cheese-and-noodle casserole she'd left for him? Or did he devour that banana pudding with a four-inch high meringue that Grandma Amanda had sent? She shook her head. *This is crazy. I have to get him out of my mind!*

She picked up the phone and punched a set of familiar numbers. "Hello, Mom. How's everybody? Yeah, I'm back...."

MONDAY MORNING she braced for the inevitable encounter with Ed. At 9:05 he called her into his office.

On his ruddy face was a forced smile, and he started out in a low, soft voice. "Look, Gwyn, I really don't care what your political affiliation is, or if you want to donate half your yearly salary to some worthy cause. What you do on your own time is your business." Placing his fists on his desk, he rose, like a monster out of the ocean. His voice grew in intensity and volume in the small, enclosed space. "But when you're representing this company, in another state, on company business, do not bring Mark Time into your little personal fight. I won't have it!"

"I'm sorry, Ed." What else could she do but agree with him? He was right. "It won't happen again."

"Is that all you have to say?"

"I have very good reasons for what I did," she countered stubbornly.

"Oh?" He sat down again and folded his arms on top of a pile of papers, his tone artificially sonorous. "Would you like to enlighten me?"

"Will you listen?"

"I'm all ears."

"I did it to help the people."

"You just couldn't keep your name out of the papers, could you?" He rolled his eyes toward the ceiling. "I can't believe you said city people weren't important."

"I didn't say that! They twisted my words. I meant that the people in Harmony Creek and on Buck Mountain are just as important as anyone in the cities!"

"Well, that's not how it sounded. Was it a thrill to see your picture on TV, knowing it was drawing nation-wide attention?"

"That's ridiculous! Surely you know that I don't care about publicity. But you must admit, it drew attention to the cause. And we got more support after that. So I'm pleased with the results."

"At least you admit it."

"Not for me. I'm really sorry Mark Time was brought into it." She sighed and gestured futilely. "Oh, Ed, I knew you wouldn't understand."

"Believe me, I'm trying."

"Let me tell you about Harmony Creek." Sponta-neously the stories just tumbled out. "There was a lit-tle girl named Emmy who needed stitches in her forehead and the mother couldn't help, so I did. I wish you could have seen how beautiful she looked after-ward, Ed, with practically no scar on her face. And an-other time, late one night, the doctor got a call to deliver twins on Buck Mountain. We had to drive through the creek because there is no bridge. Watching the birth of those twins was like seeing a miracle, right before your eyes, Ed." Her voice caught in emotion, but she cleared it and continued.

"They named the babies after us, the grandmothers, the doctor and me. Elizabeth Gwyn and Amanda Nell." She paused and smiled. "They're beautiful, healthy babies. Wish you could see them. Anyway, during the night they were born, it rained heavily, and as usually happens, Harmony Creek rose so much we couldn't drive back across it. That's why we—*they* need that bridge rebuilt.

"On the morning I was scheduled to leave, Clyde Nelson brought in his teenage son, who'd been accidentally shot in the leg while quail hunting. We couldn't leave him until the emergency helicopter arrived to fly him to the hospital in Chattanooga." She paused for a deep breath.

"Sounds like you've been doing more than organizing and setting priorities."

"I have. Believe me, Ed, I didn't do it for glory. You were right about that. I put in many long hours of hard work. It was often frustrating. But also very rewarding." She shook her head wistfully. "So much more needs to be done."

"If not for glory, Gwyn, then why?"

"I did it for—" She halted. Would he understand? Would he care? Suddenly she didn't care what he thought. Didn't care if he understood. "For love." She smiled and leaned back in her chair. "That's all I have to say."

"For love?" He looked puzzled.

She was still smiling. "Have you ever had a baby named after you, Ed?"

He shook his head.

"I hadn't, either, until last week. It gives you a sense of duty, a feeling of responsibility and a whole lot of pride."

"I have only one question, Gwyn." He gazed at her steadily. "Is it over?"

She swallowed hard but answered unequivocally. "Yes. It's over. I'm ready to go back to work in Chicago." Inside she felt sad at the admission.

"Okay, it's over." He rubbed his hands together in an act of finality. "I'll expect your report in two weeks. And I'd better not read anything in it about twins or a bridge. Now don't get me wrong. They're both well and good, but they have no place in a business report. Understand?"

"Yes, sir." She nodded and left Ed's office, thinking the spirit of Christmas must be affecting Ed because she'd gotten off easy. Maybe this confrontation was exactly what she needed to set her own mind straight. It was over, including what had happened with Neal. She just had to face that fact.

THE CHRISTMAS SEASON HAD always been a happy time for Gwyn. But this year was different. She was miserable and lonely. Although lapsing into maudlin sentimentality wasn't her style, she couldn't stop thinking about Neal. Couldn't make herself forget.

On the day she picked up the photos she'd taken in Harmony Creek, Gwyn forced herself to wait until she took a cab home before opening them. With shaky hands she examined the pictures of the smiling Hancock family.

Automatically she smiled back at W.T. and Debra, the proud parents each holding a baby. The other kids in the family clowned for the camera, and Gwyn decided right away to send copies to the Hancocks. Billy Joe, typical of a teenager trying to look gruff and remain aloof from his siblings, stood with arms folded across his chest, staring into the camera. She remembered the night he'd come after Neal, so concerned and worried about his mother when she was about to give birth.

The next photo was of Neal, leaning casually against the doorjamb, waiting for her. Was he still waiting for her? Or was it over for them? She shivered as a flood of memories left her chilled. She couldn't stop looking at him, until the tears blurred her vision and made seeing the image impossible.

On Christmas Eve she did the traditional things with her family. First, dinner with Bob and Celeste and their three kids. Then they met Angie and Andrew and attended midnight mass with their parents. On the way home it even started snowing. Big, wet flakes floated through the blackness and disappeared the minute they hit the streets. It was a beautiful night.

Gwyn tried to be happy; she could only think of Neal, however, and how much she missed him. Realistically such dreaming was a time waster. He'd already let her know he wouldn't leave the security of Harmony Creek. And she knew he couldn't abandon his responsibilities there.

She'd tried to call him today, to wish him Merry Christmas. But he wasn't home. He was probably spending a festive evening with the Nelson family, celebrating the health of their son, Kane. Or maybe he was having beef stew with Mae and Jed. Perhaps he'd driven up to Buck Mountain to spend the holiday with his namesake's family. Was he thinking of Gwyn, wishing, as she was, that they were together?

When she first stepped into the hall of her apartment building, she didn't see the dark-haired, bearded man waiting in the shadows, his broad-shouldered form silhouetted by the tiny hall light.

A movement, or a feeling, drew her gaze up from the floor. And she recognized him. *Neal!* Her step faltered, along with normal breathing. Before she could catch her breath, she was rushing toward his shadowed figure.

His shoulders were expansive in that incongruous turquoise Dolphins jacket; his waist and hips were slim in his jeans. Disheveled hair fell over his forehead; the dark beard still framed that face she'd memorized and remembered so many times. He looked tired but oh, so handsome standing there, waiting for her. Anticipation—or anxiety?—was in his weary eyes.

She wanted to touch, to kiss every inch of his face, to kiss him all over! His expression encompassed everything he was to her—strong but gentle, committed and relentless, lover and friend . . . and still vulnerable. She loved all those things about him, and more. Yes, she loved him dearly!

His mouth formed a tight line, and a muscle quirked in his jaw. But his eyes said what he couldn't. They were vibrant and smiling, almost devouring her with a closely held passion. She could feel the vibes between them as she stood before him. In those beautiful cobalt eyes she could see into his soul, see the love he so carefully hid. She read in them what she longed to know. Tonight their silent message was enough for her.

They stood there, neither one touching for long seconds. An eternity of joy and love, of longing, of resistance, of finally yielding to something stronger than either of them. She understood. That's why he was here. Resisting, and perhaps denying, was no longer possible. Oh, how she ached for him.

Neal had never seen Gwyn look more beautiful. She took his breath away. Her rich mahogany hair was pulled back, but a few capricious curls refused to obey and caught the light, creating a curious halo around her head. Her chocolate-colored eyes spoke hidden messages he couldn't understand. Or didn't want to admit. For in those eyes he saw love.

But what did he expect? He'd known it all along. Deep inside *he knew*.

"You're a little lost, aren't you?" She spoke breathlessly. "We don't often see Miami Dolphins fans around here." She touched his sleeve, sliding the satiny material between her finger and thumb, longing to touch *him*.

"I'm lost . . . without you, Gwyn."

It was what she wanted—*needed*—to hear, and she threw her arms around him, pressing her face to his chest, murmuring, "Me, too. Oh, Neal! Me, too!"

He buried his face in her hair, inhaling her honey-spiced scent, remembering how he felt with her, feeling it all over again. With a certain desperation he wanted to absorb her, to sink into the very depths of her.

Finally she looked up at him, tearful eyes smiling happily. "I'm so glad you came here, so glad to see you."

"I've missed you like crazy. Wanted to see you." His voice was husky, his desire for her clear.

"I've been to midnight mass." She chuckled self-consciously. "I prayed for . . . this. For us, Neal."

"Do you believe in answered prayers, Gwyn?"

"I do now! Let's go inside." She fumbled with her key.

Neal picked up a gift-wrapped box leaning against the wall and a gray duffel bag and followed her into the immaculate, contemporary apartment, so different from the old barracks where he lived. His gaze circled the room. "Very nice." He turned back to her. "Just what I expected you'd have."

She locked the door and stood with her back to it, unable to mask her joy at seeing him. "I can't believe you're really here."

"I'm real." He chuckled. "It's quite a trip from my neck of the woods."

She released her purse and shrugged off her coat, letting them both fall heedlessly to the floor. Moving closer, she slid her hands beneath his jacket and around his torso, her fingers exploring the muscles knitting across his back. "I'm surprised. I didn't think you'd leave Harmony Creek."

He followed her lead and let the duffel bag and box he carried slide to the floor, too. Wrapping his long arms around her, he pressed himself to her welcome warmth. "I had to see you."

She pulled back and looked at him. "I wonder if you've been as miserable as I have."

"Probably." He grinned sheepishly. "Sara and I clashed over something so insignificant I don't remember what it was. She almost quit. Mae stepped in to mediate and told me if I didn't go see you I was fired!"

Gwyn giggled and squeezed him hard. "Sounds like Harmony Creek has been less than harmonious."

"It's been awful."

"Oh, Neal, I've never felt this way with anyone before. Surely you know that." She opened his jacket and pushed it from his shoulders and down his arms. With a faint whoosh it slumped to the floor. Her eyes never left his. Again she pressed her slender form to his masculine frame and into the circle of his arms. "I can't help it, Neal. I tried not to, but . . . I love you." She lifted her face to him, inviting the kiss they both wanted.

He lowered his head, merging their lips in a hard, hungry kiss. He wanted her, perhaps more than he'd ever wanted anyone. The week since she'd left had been total misery. The unasked and unanswered questions had plagued him nightly. He had to know how she felt and to make sure about himself. Now he knew. The urgency he felt in both of them told him.

Outlining her lips with his tongue gave him instant access to her mouth. As he plunged into the sweet depths, he knew he had to have her now. With an agonized groan he let her feel the strength of his desire.

She reached for the bottom edge of his sweater and shoved the garment up his chest. While he pulled it over his head, she peeled off her own red sweater. Feverishly she helped him unbutton his shirt. Impatiently she tugged it from his waistband. "I want to touch you. Make sure you're real."

When she unzipped his slacks, Neal thought he'd die if he couldn't have her *now*. "Oh, I am! I want you, Gwyn."

With a feverish blur of activity they finished undressing right there in her foyer, leaving their clothes in rumpled heaps on the floor. When they were nude, they came together in a heated passion that surpassed anything either of them had ever known. The act encompassed the desperate feelings of being alone, the questions of loyalty, of love, and the joys of shared passion and being together again.

She clasped his shoulders and pulled herself to meet his kiss, to align their bodies. He placed his hands beneath her buttocks and lifted her up so she could wrap her legs around his hips. Clinging and writhing, she sparred teasingly with him, relishing the feel of his aroused masculine pleasure.

He moaned and tore his lips away, feeling quite desperate to complete their union. "Gwyn—"

"The sofa," she whispered.

He lowered her to the cushions and hovered only a moment before seeking the warm union they both desired. "I've dreamed about this moment a thousand times this past week. Dreamed of you, Gwyn."

"Come on. Hurry. . ." she begged.

With hands and hips in motion she met his rocking rhythm and countered his urgency with her own. As their bodies conveyed messages of desire, their spirits merged with undeniable signals of love. They reached the crest and soared beyond, the meanings unclear and unnecessary at the moment, but signatures of love nonetheless. These memories of uncontrolled passion would remain as testament to their love.

Later, in the quiet, contented moments of recovery, he kissed her tenderly. "Not too spontaneous, I hope."

"Not everything has to be planned." She sighed and stroked his back.

"Like this visit? I tried to call you tonight and tell you I was on my way."

"I was with my family all evening. I only regret I couldn't have met you at the airport."

"I'm not even sure I understand why I did this."

"I think I do." She kissed the hairy mat on his chest. She felt as if she knew a secret about Neal that he didn't know. Actually it was because he wouldn't admit it. But in time . . . maybe . . . "I'm curious. How did you get a flight this late?"

"From an independent dealer's ad in the Chattanooga paper." He sighed. "I had to see you again, even if it meant leaving Harmony Creek. Had to touch you. And love you."

"I was convinced you wouldn't leave Harmony Creek."

"It's about time, don't you think?" He scooted to his side and cuddled her in his arms, squeezing her to him on the narrow sofa. "I couldn't stay alone for the holidays again. I figured I'd better start making some better memories for myself."

"Oh, Neal, I do love you." Joy swelled in her heart, and she leaned forward to kiss him, letting her lips reinforce her vows of love.

THEY AWOKE the next morning to four inches of snow. It was the perfect Christmas Day. They fixed French toast for breakfast and took it back to her bedroom to eat it in bed. When they finished, Neal insisted that she open the Christmas present he'd brought.

"But, Neal, I didn't get you a gift."

"I didn't get you one, either. Not actually. I'm just the delivery boy. This is from Kane Nelson's grandmother. She wanted to thank you for everything you did for her grandson. And for me."

"For you? What does she know about that?"

"She knows I'm smiling at odd times. She just doesn't know exactly why, but I'll bet she could figure it out without much effort. Hurry up and open it."

Laughing with a youthful eagerness, Gwyn tore open the box and lifted out the soft, handmade gift. With both hands she carefully extended the white, crocheted triangular shawl with long fringe on two sides. Tiny ecru seed pearls had been sewn into the delicate shell designs. "Why, it's absolutely beautiful!" She stretched the exquisite garment out at arm's length. "Oh, Neal! This is one of the most lovely things I've ever seen. It's . . . it's worth a fortune!"

"So are you, Gwyn, darling. To all of us in Harmony Creek. Put it on."

She wrapped the shawl around her shoulders, and immediately its beauty enhanced the skimpy lavender nightgown she wore.

"Wear it like this." He pulled the nightgown's spaghetti straps off her shoulders and scooted the silky garment down her body. When she was completely nude, he carefully draped the white shawl around her.

"I don't think Grandma Nelson had this in mind," Gwyn said with a devilish laugh.

"Who knows?" He chuckled and laid her back against the pillows. She was a picture of erotic beauty, all dark and light, with tiny patches of silky skin visible beneath the intricate lace shells. "But it's what I had in mind from the minute I saw the gift she'd made for you. I knew you'd like it. And that I'd love you in it." He kissed her, then leaned back to admire her feminine beauty.

The shawl molded to her curves, caressing the swells of her breasts, not quite hiding her taut nipples. Their roseate tips peeked through the lace and contrasted with the creamy pearls sprinkled over the creation. The long fringe teased her belly button and crisscrossed the mahogany curls at the crest of her femininity.

Neal played the sensuous game as long as he could before he took her, pressing himself to her shawl-embraced body. "Merry Christmas, my beautiful Gwyn."

"Yes, it is. Merry Christmas, my love." She gathered him to her, receiving the male strength he had to offer, giving of herself and her love.

"Indeed, yes..."

LATER THAT DAY Gwyn took Neal to her parents' for Christmas dinner. The family was a bit surprised to be meeting this man she'd so recently met in Tennessee. They were polite and somewhat reserved at first, but before the day was over, he'd won their approval. It was hard for anyone not to like Neal.

The lovers spent three glorious days and nights together, exploring Gwyn's world in the Windy City and making love. But when Neal left for Harmony Creek, they still hadn't come to any solutions to their ultimate dilemma. They both had commitments that didn't include such a drastic change in life-styles.

Another obstacle remained. Although Gwyn had declared her love for him, Neal had not committed himself to that extent. She assumed he couldn't say it. Not yet.

And in the back of her mind she feared...maybe not ever.

12

"CAN I BE HONEST with you, Doc?"

"Sure, Mae. Why not?"

"You might not like what I have to say." She leaned closer and scrutinized Neal's eyes. "Bloodshot. Dark circles. You look like something the cat dragged in and the dog wouldn't have."

Neal burst into laughter. "Well, you're certainly candid."

"You wanted honesty." She set a closed plastic container on the table along with a smaller foil-wrapped package. "I do believe you're losing weight, too."

"Isn't that what everyone's trying to do?"

"Not around here. Maybe city folks are." She motioned to the container. "I've been worried about you, Doc. That's why I brought you this stew."

"Thank you, Mae."

"There's some corn bread, too. Be sure and eat all of it."

"I certainly will." He smiled. "Thanks."

"Don't mention it." She pulled out a chair. "Mind if I have a seat?"

"No, please go ahead."

"You know, you just can't let yourself get sick. Too many folks around here depend on you."

"I'm not getting sick." He grabbed the container of stew and stuffed it in the refrigerator. "Don't worry about me, Mae. I'm just fine. I'm the physician, re-member?"

"Then, 'physician, heal thyself,'" she said sharply, quoting the Bible.

He looked at her quickly. "What's that supposed to mean?"

"Something's wrong, Doc. You look awful and act . . . well, let's just say you're not the nicest sort these days."

"Sorry. I guess I'm just working too hard."

"Then take a little time off, like you did at Christmas. Go to . . . Chicago."

He shook his head.

"I do declare, you look a little peaked. Does it have something to do with that cute little gal who whipped the office into shape?"

He winced and shook his head. "I . . . I don't know."

"Well, she did a great job everywhere. But she sure left you in sad shape."

"Now, Mae—"

She held up her wrinkled hand. "You can say I'm an interfering ol' woman if you want to, but I think this whole mess revolves around her."

Neal grinned. "I might agree that you're somewhat interfering, but I'd never call you an ol' woman, Mae."

"You know just what to say, don't you, Doc? I think you're avoiding the subject. The subject of you and a pretty gal named Gwyn Frederick."

"Now you are interfering, Mae." He folded his arms across his chest. "You don't know the whole story."

"I know what I see in your eyes. And I remember how hers sparkled when she looked at you."

"There are no easy solutions to this."

"There never are when it comes to matters of the heart. Don't you know that by now?"

"Yeah, I guess."

"I think you've been bit by the love bug, Doc."

He gazed steadily at her for a moment, then turned away with a heavy sigh. "Okay, Mae, I'll be honest with you. Sure, I'm attracted to her. But I don't know whether it's love." He paused and looked back at her. "Or lust."

She met his gaze just as steadily, not letting his choice of words get to her. "Well, sir, I guess you won't know until love hits you in the head. But this time I think it punched you in the stomach."

He nodded. "I'll keep that in mind."

"Does she love you?"

"She says so."

"Then why doesn't she hightail it down here?"

He shrugged. "I can't ask her to leave everything in her life and come to Harmony Creek."

"Why not?"

"There isn't anything here for her."

"There's you." Mae shook her head and stood. "In my day, love was enough." She headed for the door. "'Course, you've got to know your own heart. And tell her so. I suspect that's what she's waiting on."

Neal stared at the door after Mae left. He knotted his fist and pounded the table. Then he paced the room, muttering unintelligible curses. When pacing wasn't enough, he decided to go jogging. But a heavy sweat didn't bring solutions.

Late that night, when he couldn't sleep, he came to a solid deduction. Mae was right. First he had to know his own heart. And right now, he'd give anything to see Gwyn, to hold her again. To tell her of his love.

GWYN STARED at the newspaper article. It was a tiny item, hidden on the next-to-back page of the sports section. It wasn't big news, certainly not to anyone in Chicago. Only to her. But it was very important to the people of Harmony Creek.

Signed petitions requesting the rebuilding of a bridge over flood-prone Harmony Creek would be presented to the legislature, and the protest would culminate in a march on the capitol. The event would show the substantial numbers of supporters for the "bridge to nowhere." As she read the article, Gwyn was filled with pride for the fighting spirit of the people in Harmony Creek, folks she had grown to love. And she wanted to champion their efforts in some way.

She wanted to participate.

Heart pounding, Gwyn realized she longed to march up those capitol steps, proving that she cared by her presence. More than that, she wanted to walk beside Neal.

But how could she arrange it? Ed had made her situation perfectly clear. Stay out of it! This wasn't her fight. It definitely wasn't her business. Reluctantly she had agreed. Until now.

The more Gwyn thought about it, the more convinced she became that attending the march was the excuse she needed to see Neal again.

TWO DAYS LATER Gwyn Frederick stood in Tennessee, squinting in the Nashville sun. A surprisingly large crowd had gathered on the capitol steps. It looked as if all of Harmony Creek, Murphy and the surrounding mountain communities had turned out for the occasion.

Everyone but Neal.

As she searched the crowd for one tall, dark-haired doctor, she felt strangely sure of herself, especially considering the fact that she had committed an act of insubordination that would surely cost her her job.

"Gwyn! Gwyn Frederick!"

She whirled around at the sound of her name, then waved when she spotted two familiar faces beaming at her as they approached. "Mae! Jed! Great to see you!" She hugged them both.

"I'm so glad you decided to come, Gwyn." Mae smiled at Gwyn with a special gleam in her eyes. "Neal will be, too."

"Is he here?"

"He had an emergency, as usual. Had to take a few stitches. But I'm sure he'll be here."

Gwyn nodded and acted calm. But inside her heart was going crazy. She hadn't realized how anxious she was to see him.

They waved at the Hancocks, parents of the twins. Then the entire Nelson family including Kane, who'd been shot, came over for a greeting. Gwyn's anxiety was growing as more Harmony Creek residents came over to shake her hand. Where was Neal? Maybe he wasn't going to make it.

Maybe she wouldn't see him at all. Her heart sank at the thought.

"It's about time to start. Where *is* that doc?" Mae asked, voicing the frustration Gwyn was feeling. "There's Representative Sanders. He's going to lead the march."

As the crowd of several hundred began to move into more orderly lines, Gwyn felt panicky. What if Neal didn't make it? She realized now that he was the reason she was here. He was all she cared about. And he was tearing her heart apart.

Suddenly she saw him.

A tall, dark-haired man with a beard was maneuvering through the crowd. Toward her. Gwyn's heart pounded like a pair of bongos, and when he stood before her, his blue eyes expressive and shining, she thought she would burst into happy tears.

"Gwyn—" was all he managed before sweeping her into his arms.

The crowd forgotten, she was alone with him, engulfed in the utter, complete happiness of being with Neal. He pressed her to his chest, allowing their two hearts to beat together. In that glorious moment her mission was complete. *This* was where she belonged. In Neal's embrace.

Finally Neal held her at arm's length and looked closely into her eyes. His were dancing with happiness. "Aren't you a little lost? We don't usually have out-of-town supporters of local causes. It's risky for a city gal like you."

She smiled happily up at him. "The risk is worth it for this moment alone. This is exactly where I belong, Neal. With you."

"I like your priorities. But wouldn't you rather wait in my Jeep until this is over?"

"Why in the world would I want to do that?"

He shrugged. "To stay out of sight."

"I'm not hiding anymore, Neal."

"According to Ed, maybe you should."

"Ed? What's he got to do with this?"

"He called my office this morning, trying to find you. I had the distinct feeling he wanted to prevent your involvement in today's event."

"It's too late. I'm here. And I'm staying." She clasped his hand firmly in hers. "I'm here to march.'"

He tucked both of her hands to his chest. "Gwyn, I have to tell you—" Someone in the crowd jostled them, and he pulled her protectively to him. "Over here." He steered her away from the street and up on the curb.

"Can it wait, Neal?"

"No, this can't wait another minute. I'm afraid I've waited too long now." His hands gripped her shoulders firmly. "Gwyn, I love you. I love you more than anything in my life. And nothing—not my past, not my job or yours—nothing will come between us. We'll work it out and do whatever it takes."

She smiled up at him, her heart singing, her eyes brimming with tears. "I love you, too, Neal. With all my heart." Gwyn had never been happier. "And I have no doubts about our love, Neal. I've known for a long time how you felt in your heart. But I just had to wait until you could see it."

"You're very perceptive, Ms Frederick."

"I'm very much in love, Doctor."

"So am I." He encircled her in his arms and kissed her, long and hard, right there near the crowd on the capitol steps. The love in his heart was obvious for all to see.

They didn't stop kissing until they heard an uproarious noise and looked up to see the entire throng of marchers cheering for them. They beamed and waved and joined the crowd.

After the march and presentation of the petitions to the governor, they drove back to East Tennessee in a long caravan. Neal gave several people a ride, so there was no opportunity for privacy with Gwyn until they arrived at the clinic where he lived. When they were in bed, he tucked her into his arms.

"Okay, young lady. You have some explaining to do."

She snuggled down with him, burying her face against his chest and inhaling his wonderful deep-woods scent. "After."

"Now."

Her hand trailed the dark hairline of his torso. "Later," she whispered, touching him intimately.

He grabbed her hand and pinned it to the pillow above her head. "Gwyn," he muttered roughly. "Talk to me."

"I love you, Neal. I'm here to stay. It's that simple."

"And that complex." His face tightened; his blue eyes grew smoky with passion. "You understand I have a commitment here for another year."

"Yes."

"I don't want you going back to Chicago. I know it sounds selfish, but I want you here with me. So I can love you every day."

"Me, too, Neal. That's why I'm here."

"Are you sure you're willing to leave your family and job and everything you hold dear?"

"You are the one I hold most dear, Neal." With her free hand she ran her fingers through his hair, cupping the back of his head and pulling him down to her for another thorough kiss. "I love you with all my heart and soul, Neal. You're like no other man I've ever met. And I want to spend my time—my life—with you."

He sighed and his voice was a sweet whisper. "Gwyn, I love you so much it hurts to imagine being without you again. I can say it now, from my heart. And I'm ready to give you all the love you can handle." He kissed her tenderly, then brushed her bare breasts lightly with his beard as he moved over her, kissing certain sensi-

tive places. "I want to give you all the love you can
stand, and then some."

"Oh, Neal..." She gasped with delight as his lips
teased her erotically.

With renewed joy and commitment Gwyn opened
her heart and her body to the man she loved. She had
come here today because she couldn't hold back her
love any longer, even though she wasn't sure he could
admit his true feelings. But she had shown herself to be
willing to sacrifice everything for him. Now there
would be no waiting, no holding back. They could love
freely, with no barriers.

One moment, though, would stay with Gwyn forever. When Neal had told her of his love today on the
capitol steps, she could swear she'd seen tears in his deep
blue eyes.

They rode together to love's summit, each express-
ing a new and endearing depth of love. And as Gwyn
settled in Neal's arms for the night, she felt his love
reaching out to her, encircling her, giving her strength
and happiness. And she had never felt more sure about
anything—or anyone—in her life.

THE NEXT EVENING at the McPhersons' Representative
Sanders settled the affair of the bridge. He stood on a
kitchen step stool and raised both hands for attention.
"Ladies and gentlemen, I have some good news. Some
very good news. The governor has assured me that the
flood relief money will indeed be allocated to the rebuilding of the bridge to Buck Mountain! After all our
hard work, we won!"

There was an uproar of loud cheering from the
twenty or so friends gathered in the large living room.

Representative Sanders raised his hands for quiet again. "Now, now, hold it down. I've been asked to make another announcement. And I'm almost as proud to make this one as the first." He paused for emphasis and let his smile sweep the crowd, then rest on Neal and Gwyn. "It's my pleasure to announce the upcoming nuptials of Dr. Neal Perry and Ms Gwyn Frederick. And you're all invited to the wedding!"

The crowd responded with applause and happy exclamations.

Neal stood with his arm around Gwyn and smiled proudly. When the group quieted, he spoke to them. "The ceremony will be here at Mae and Jed's next Sunday afternoon. And if everybody will bring a dish, we'll have a little party. Several of you already know some of my favorites."

"Are you taking a honeymoon?" someone in the crowd asked.

"Our plans aren't firm, but I suspect we'll take a few days to be alone. Don't worry about the clinic, though. I'll request a substitute physician."

"Are you coming back?" someone else asked. For a moment there was dead silence in the rowdy, happy group.

Gwyn and Neal exchanged glances, and she lifted her head and faced the crowd. "Of course we'll be back. We both have lots of work to do at Harmony Creek Clinic."

An audible sigh of relief rippled through the group.

"I'd like to make a special request," Gwyn continued. "Would those of you bringing the doctor's favorite dishes also bring me the recipes? I want to learn how to cook for my husband."

Everyone laughed and cheered and someone pulled out some cherished bottles of blackberry wine to toast the successes of the day.

Neal's arm tightened around Gwyn's shoulders. He tipped his glass toward hers. "To our share of the glory, darling. May we always be this happy."

She smiled and leaned into the secure circle of his embrace. "To us. Not for glory, Neal. Only for love." She touched her glass to his. "May our love be this glorious forever."

COMING NEXT MONTH

#245 A BRIGHT IDEA Gina Wilkins

Brooke Matheny knew exactly what she wanted from
marriage, and chose a suitable candidate
accordingly. Only problem was, the man rejected her
proposal. But when Matthew James overheard
Brooke's proposition, he had no qualms at all about
inviting Brooke to continue the conversation—
with *him*.

#246 ANOTHER HEAVEN Renee Roszel

The moment Rule Danforth and his crazy relatives
set foot on Barren Heath Island, Mandy McRae knew
things would never be the same. Yet her philosophy
was if you can't beat 'em, join 'em, which is how she
became Rule's partner in a bizarre treasure
hunt . . . and other even more rewarding pursuits!

#247 THE COLOR OF LOVE Binnie Syril

Since she'd learned to live in the darkness, Judith
Blake couldn't bear the thought of the man who'd
ruined her career as an artist. Then Mark Leland
reentered her life, shattering her cocoon but giving
her colors she'd never been able to see before. . . .

#248 A NOVEL APPROACH
Emma Jane Spenser

It wasn't until Adam had witnessed three "murders,"
perpetrated by one Danielle Courtland, that he
realized he was in love with a pseudokiller. And even
after he'd discovered the reason behind her bizarre
behavior, Dani continued to make him feel as though
he'd just stepped through the looking glass. . . .